the new guy

(AND OTHER

SENIOR YEAR

DISTRACTIONS)

AMY SPALDING

POPPY
LITTLE,
BROWN

Little, Brown and Company
New York   Boston

Poppy

Hachette Book Group
1290 Avenue of the Americas, New York, NY 10104
Visit us at lb-teens.com

Poppy is an imprint of Little, Brown and Company.
The Poppy name and logo are trademarks of Hachette Book Group, Inc.

The publisher is not responsible for websites (or their content) that are not owned by the publisher.

First Edition: April 2016

Library of Congress Cataloging-in-Publication Data

Names: Spalding, Amy, author.
 Title: The new guy (and other senior year distractions) / by Amy Spalding.
 Description: First edition. | New York ; Boston : Little, Brown and Company, 2016. | "Poppy." | Summary: "Juggling the pressures of college applications and friendships, neurotic overachiever Jules's plans for her senior year are thrown off track when she starts dating the new guy at school and finds herself at the center of a rivalry between her high school's newspaper and its just-launched TV news show"— Provided by publisher.
 Identifiers: LCCN 2015021419| ISBN 9780316382786 (hardback) | ISBN 9780316382762 (ebook) | ISBN 9780316382793 (library edition ebook)
 Subjects: | CYAC: High schools—Fiction. | Schools—Fiction. | Dating (Social customs)—Fiction. | Competition (Psychology)—Fiction. | Fame—Fiction. | Los Angeles (Calif.)—Fiction. | BISAC: JUVENILE FICTION / Girls & Women. | JUVENILE FICTION / Humorous Stories. | JUVENILE FICTION / Love & Romance. | JUVENILE FICTION / Social Issues / Dating & Sex. | JUVENILE FICTION / Social Issues / Friendship.
 Classification: LCC PZ7.S73189 New 2016 | DDC [Fic]—dc23 LC record available at http://lccn.loc.gov/2015021419

10 9 8 7 6 5 4 3 2 1

RRD-C

Printed in the United States of America

To my friend Nadia Osman

Every day I C U in the hall

C U drinking coffee @ the mall

Every day I fall and fall

More in <3 with U

But each time I C U passing by

I get tongue-tied cuz I'm way 2 shy

Ur so special and I don't know Y

I just can't say 2 U

Want 2 B Ur Boy

Want 2 C U smile

Want 2 hold Ur hand

And hang out 4 a while

Want 2 B the 1

Ur 2 good 2 B true

Hope U want me 2 B Ur boy 2

—Chaos 4 All, "Want 2 B Ur Boy"

CHAPTER ONE

Even though it's only the second day of my senior year, the routine's familiar. When a new student starts at Eagle Vista Academy, one of us gives them a quick tour and at least the illusion of a friendly face in the crowd. The school is expensive, so I think the Reception Committee is an attempt to make new kids tell their parents they were warmly welcomed. Parents therefore immediately feel like they got their money's worth.

I joined the Reception Committee when I was a freshman, so I've done this more times than I can count. I'm notified a day in advance to be at the guidance office before first period begins, and when I show up, I get the new student's schedule.

But this morning is not like any of the other mornings.

To be fair, it wasn't to begin with. We have our first meeting of the *Crest* after school, and Mr. Wheeler will announce who's been selected as newspaper editor in chief. If it's not me...well, I can't think about that outcome right now.

Needless to say, I'm in no shape to be the best possible liaison a new student deserves.

Much less this new student.

Though maybe it isn't him. There must be other Alex Powells besides *the* Alex Powell.

Ms. Guillory, the guidance administrator, clears her throat. I look over to her and realize I may have been zoning out for more than a split second.

"Of course we pride ourselves on all students enjoying an excellent but typical high school experience here," she says. "But with some students, it's important we pay *special* attention to that."

I know then that it *is* the Alex Powell.

"I'll be back on time," I promise her as I dash out of the office. Luckily my best friend, Sadie, is at her locker when I run up.

"You look panicked," she says.

"Look at this." I hold up my liaison packet right in her face. "Look at it, Sadie. Don't read it out loud, but *look at it.*"

"Oh my god," she says. The packet's still in her face, so she's a little muffled. "Alex Powell."

"I said not to read it out loud."

"Jules, you should know I can't follow a command like that. Wait, so do we know if it's *the* Alex Powell?"

"Stop saying his name," I whisper. "And, yes. I think so, at least. I don't have one hundred percent confirmation yet."

"Can you imagine?" Sadie checks her reflection in her

locker mirror and fluffs her violet hair. "One day you're one-fifth of the biggest boy band in the country, and then—how many years later? Two?"

"Two," I say. Two years ago, it felt as if you couldn't go anywhere without hearing "Want 2 B Ur Boy." Two years ago, everyone knew Chaos 4 All. Two years ago, Alex Powell was *famous.*

"Jules, this is a big responsibility," Sadie says. "You are welcoming a teen idol to our school."

"He's not a teen idol anymore," I say. There'd been at least a couple of songs after "Want 2 B Ur Boy," but they hadn't been so universally beloved. And then it was like Chaos 4 All had never even existed.

"Mom says once you're famous, you're changed," Sadie says. "For good."

Sadie's parents are actors, so her mom would know.

"I have to go," I say. "I can't be late to welcome him. I should never be late to welcome someone on their first day, but—"

"But especially not Alex Powell," she says. "Go."

I rush back to the guidance office, where I appear to have beaten Alex Powell. I've been trying to picture him, but in my head he's still fifteen with perfectly floppy hair straight out of a photo shoot.

"Welcome back, Miss McAllister-Morgan," Ms. Guillory says with a sigh, and I think I'm supposed to realize I shouldn't have dashed off, even briefly. It probably wasn't the most professional move, but today shouldn't call for standard operating procedures.

All right, of course today should. That's why standard operating procedures *exist*.

"And good morning, Mr. Powell," Ms. Guillory says, looking past me.

I turn my head very slowly in a calculated swivel.

Alex Powell, *the* Alex Powell, is standing right inside the swinging doors.

"Good morning," he says with a little grin.

Great. Just *great*. He's still cute. He's not floppy-hair-straight-out-of-a-photo-shoot cute, but real-life cute instead.

And real-life cute is so much better.

"You're in good hands," Ms. Guillory tells him with a little gesture to me. "Good luck on your first day."

She takes a seat and looks to her computer, and normally this is when I jump in seamlessly. But I'm still marveling that he's here.

"Hey," he says to me, and I try to reconcile the famous fifteen-year-old with the person standing in front of me, who seems now like he'd want to be someone's *man*, not their boy.

Oh my god, why am I thinking stuff like this *like I know him*? Seeing someone on TV and the Internet doesn't equal knowing him. We're *strangers*.

He's tall—I'm bad with guessing heights, but I think over six feet—and he's filled out. His dark hair used to be styled very precisely. Now it's grown out just a little, and a wavy chunk falls over his forehead in a way that makes me want to lean over and brush it back.

Oh my god, Jules, no! Do not think of touching Alex, his hair, or his forehead. You're a professional. Professionals keep their hands to themselves, even inside their brains.

"Miss McAllister-Morgan," says Ms. Guillory, and now I wonder if I was just standing there gaping at Alex Powell.

When you live in LA, people being famous isn't the biggest deal. There are Sadie's parents, of course, and a few kids show up only toward the end of the year when their TV shows aren't shooting, and Nick Weber was on a Disney show as the annoying little brother back in grade school. But the TV kids only talk to me if they're talking to Sadie, and I've barely spoken to Nick at all.

And yet now I have to speak to Alex. I have to speak to Alex *with authority*. Because I'm on the Eagle Vista Academy Reception Committee. I'm the vice president of the Eagle Vista Academy Reception Committee.

"Hi, I'm Jules McAllister-Morgan. I'm your Eagle Vista Academy Reception Committee liaison. What's your name?"

Obviously the question is not one I need to ask.

"Alex," he says with a broad smile that takes over his entire face. "Alex Powell. Thanks."

I take that in like new information.

"Nice to meet you, Alex." I pause to beam my practiced welcome smile. I've learned from mainlining *America's Next Top Model* marathons with my friends that the giveaway of

5

a fake smile is not involving your eyes, so I make sure mine crinkle up a little.

In general—not just with my expression—I think it's incredibly important to project the right image. Since today I was on liaison duty and I'm awaiting the newspaper editor announcement, I made sure to wear one of my more professional outfits. My structured gray top goes perfectly with the subtle floral pattern on my A-line skirt, and because my black flats are brand-new, there's not even the hint of a scuff on them yet. My blond hair is pulled back into a low ponytail, not only to keep it out of my face but also to give the impression I don't care about frivolous things like my hair.

"I'll take you around so you'll know where your classes are," I continue. "It can be a little confusing with a few in different buildings."

"Okay, cool," he says, even though nothing having to do with the Eagle Vista Academy Reception Committee could realistically be taken as *cool*. "Here's my schedule."

He starts to hand it over, but I hold up my copy. "Part of the job."

"You're very prepared," he says in a voice that almost sounds like flirtation. So I remind myself of who I'm dealing with here. This is *Alex Powell*. Alex Powell probably has developed flirtation superpowers. Maybe Alex Powell was born with flirtation superpowers.

The voice has nothing to do with me.

"So you've got calculus first hour—that's in Maywood Hall,

the main academic building, through the courtyard. Most of your classes are in there; let me show you."

He falls into step beside me as we walk out of the tiny administrative building and into the open courtyard. People make fun of the cliché of Los Angeles weather, but if you lived anywhere else, you'd have to feel jealous at least sometimes, wouldn't you? The sky is clear, and the sun shines down in golden rays, and it's as if the whole city wants to welcome Alex.

I do not blame the city.

"What year are you?" he asks.

"I'm a senior too. So Maywood Hall is the middle building; you just have to make a right and follow that path." I take a couple of steps ahead of him while pointing it out. "We can go in, but we have to stay pretty quiet."

"I can manage that," he says.

I hold open one heavy front door for him. He kind of brushes against me as he walks in, and while it's not the most boy contact I've ever had, it's close. It feels like a lot out of nowhere. Maybe it's why I forget to keep moving, and that's definitely why the hem of my skirt gets sucked in as the door swings shut.

"*No!*" I shout, even though it's too late.

Alex cocks one of his eyebrows. The move pulls his whole face into a smile. "What about staying quiet?"

I try to pull away from the door, but the door is stronger, and I can feel the waistband doing its best to pull down away from my waist. And I definitely do not want Alex Powell to see my underwear at all, but especially not today because tonight is Laundry Night. That means I am wearing my least favorite pair, which are pink-and-black leopard print, like my butt is a 1980s rock star. I only own them because Mom still holds out hope I'm secretly as cool as she is.

I think both Mom and I know the truth by now: I am not.

"Don't move." Alex swoops back in and throws open the door. My skirt does get displaced, but I'm almost positive I fix it in time to keep him from seeing even the tiniest sliver of hot pink and black.

Almost.

"You didn't warn me how dangerous it is here," Alex says.

"There's actually nearly a zero percent crime rate on school grounds," I say.

"I was kidding," he says with a smile.

I check that his eyes are crinkled to see if it's a real smile, and they are, so it is. I can't believe Alex Powell is smiling at me. Technically, I guess Alex Powell is smiling at my dorkiness in the face of my Great Skirt Emergency, but it's still a smile of his directed at me.

"Sorry, I know, I mean, I should have known." I hear my voice and how I just sound like Regular Jules now, not at all like Eagle Vista Academy Reception Committee Vice President Jules. Time to reset. "There's a stairwell at each end of the main corridor. For some reason, freshmen clog up the right one, so I'd suggest using the left one when you can. Let's head back out so I can show you the other main academic building."

"Be careful this time," he says as I open the door. "This building clearly wants to feed on your clothes."

"Ha-ha," I say. *Ha-ha?* I meant to actually laugh!

"Hey, Jules? That's your name, right? It's Jules?"

"It's Jules, yes."

"Anyway." Alex stops walking for a moment and shrugs. Because he's so tall, I have to look up to watch the shrugging. "You can go ahead and say it if you want."

"Say what?" I ask, even though of course I know what he means. How would I even do that, if I deemed it polite? *Hey, didn't you used to be famous? Hey, do u still want 2 B anyone's boy?*

He exhales audibly. "I—never mind."

"Changing schools must be hard," I say, even though Ms. Guillory says we should never emphasize the bad parts of switching schools, only the fun ones, and even though I'm nearly positive that isn't what Alex means.

"I've done it a few times," he says. "It's not that big a deal. It's still the first week, only Tuesday. Could be worse."

"You're brave," I say without thinking. It earns me another real smile, though.

"Thanks for the tour," he says, "Jules."

Really and truly, I know this isn't actual flirting. But also really and truly, I like it anyway.

I show him Fair Park Building and the Mount Royal Building for the Arts, then walk him into the cafeteria. I explain where the various lines—entrées, salad bar, grill, smoothies—are, and then I circle him back to the administrative wing and explain how he can go to his advisor for anything he needs. This is always the last step of the tour—and usually by now I'm feeling that twinge of *I should get to class so I don't miss anything else*—but right now I wish the tour had several more attractions.

"So I hope that you've gotten an idea of how the school's laid out, and where to find anything you need," I say with my practiced smile. "And, again, you can always contact your advisor or any Eagle Vista Academy Reception Committee liaison."

"Like you," he says.

"Like me," I say, dismissing the warmth or whatever tone his voice sounds washed in. "I'm vice president, so I'm always available to help."

"That's a big responsibility," he says. The tone is still there. "If the president dies, you've got to step up."

I already barely know how flirting works unless I'm observing others, but then throw *Alex Powell* into the mix? I literally just stand there, again, staring at him.

I do decide, however, that it's marginally better than saying *ha-ha* again.

"Thanks for the tour," he tells me.

"Part of the job," I say, again, and even though I think I'm just going to inwardly cringe, I outwardly cringe a little too. Get it together, Jules! "Good luck."

CHAPTER TWO

The spot next to Sadie in women's history is, of course, open for me, and I slip as quietly into the room as I can manage. I don't know why I bother, because I'm still getting out my textbook and notebook when she throws her pen at me.

"Was it him?" she whispers, if you can call it that. Sadie's volume only seems to turn down so far.

I nod and keep my attention on my desk, even though I can't wait to share everything with her.

"What was he like?"

"Miss Sheraton-Hayes." Ms. Cannon doesn't even bother to hide a sigh. "If you'd like to talk to Miss McAllister-Morgan, might I suggest after class or at lunch?"

"Great ideas," Sadie says, somehow not sounding sarcastic even though no one else could pull off that feat. "Sorry, Ms. Cannon."

I wait until we're in the hallway after class to broach the subject. "He was actually—"

"Hang on." Sadie's attention is completely on her phone. "Everyone's texting. Did you get a picture of him?"

"*A picture?*"

"With your phone?"

"I couldn't take a picture of"—I stop myself and drop my voice to a whisper, a real whisper, not a Sadie-style one—"Alex Powell with my phone."

"Jules!" She swats me on the arm. "What good is it having my best friend on the Reception Committee if it doesn't benefit me in any way?"

"It's really not supposed to benefit you in any way," I say.

"He's in Em's calculus class," Sadie says. "Imagine being in calculus, doing calculus stuff, with *Alex Powell.*"

I check my phone as well, even though that's against Eagle Vista Academy rules. There's nothing about today that doesn't feel like an exception. "Em just texted. She says that no one is making a big deal out of him being here. Maybe people don't really remember."

"It was only two years ago," Sadie says. "Wait! Why am I checking in with Em? I haven't even debriefed you yet!"

"I have to get to class," I say. "I haven't even been to my locker yet."

"This is totally worth being late for," Sadie says, but I fear tardy slips far more than Sadie does, so we split up for now. Em's in my Latin class, which is my next class, and she raises her eyebrows at me as I sit down.

"You heard, I assume," she says. "Or you checked your texts for once."

"Yes and yes," I say. "I was his liaison this morning."

"He seems normal," she says.

"Completely. He was really nice."

"And hot," she says. "Very hot."

"I didn't notice," I say for some reason, and Em's eyebrows find new heights. "No, I noticed. Obviously I noticed. I don't know why I said I didn't."

"Because you're a professional, and you take your liaison duties very seriously."

I'm pretty sure Em's being sarcastic, but it's true that I do.

♥ ♥ ♥

"Jules, will you ever forgive us?" Sadie deposits a cupcake on top of my notebook before sitting down next to me at our lunch table. "In the Alex excitement, you were totally forgotten."

"Nah, Jules is never forgotten," Sadie's boyfriend, Justin, says.

"They're choosing newspaper editor today," Sadie says. "You're not worried, are you? You're obviously getting it."

"I'm not obviously getting it," I say as Em and her boyfriend, Thatcher, sit down. "Natalie could get it."

"Pffffff, Natalie." Sadie waves this absolutely true possibility off with a flick of her wrist. "Wheeler would be insane to pick her."

"He wouldn't be," I say, because we are as evenly matched as two competitors can be. We both have perfect GPAs, we've both been on the honor roll throughout high school, and we both have a solid mix of extracurriculars. "But thank you for the cupcake."

"Is there just one cupcake?" Thatcher asks with hope in his eyes.

There is, but I split it with him mainly because I don't want to make him sad but also because maybe karma will reward my generosity with the editor position. I'm not entirely sure if that's how karma works, but I'm willing to sacrifice half a cupcake to find out.

We used to share a bigger table with a bigger group of girls, but then people started getting boyfriends, and friends of boyfriends started joining in. So instead of being clustered together at one of the long tables, the huge group split up among the smaller round tables on the other side of the cafeteria. Now it's just Sadie and her boyfriend, Em and her boyfriend, and me. I've decided it's for the best that boys can't be my focus right now, because this smaller table comfortably seats five. A boy wouldn't just be crammed into my way-too-busy life; he'd have to be crammed into the seating arrangement as well.

"Hey, Jules?"

I look up to see that Alex Powell is standing near our table. Very near. Other tables have noticed too. It feels as if more than half the cafeteria is looking our way. But I think it feels that way because, literally, more than half the cafeteria is looking our way.

"Hi," I say in perfect liaison tone. "Do you need any help navigating the cafeteria?"

"No," he says, and smiles. Actually, he's already smiling, but he smiles more. Alex's smile possibilities seem vast and unending. "I navigated it pretty well. Cool if I..."

He nods at the table, and of course on one hand it's obvious what he's suggesting. But on the other, I cannot believe this is what he is suggesting, so I don't say anything.

"Sit down," Sadie tells him. "Justin, get him a chair."

"You don't have to sit with me because I'm your liaison," I say. "There aren't any liaison rules about lunches or anything. There are barely any liaison rules at all."

"Jules, stop saying *liaison*," Em says.

Justin returns with a chair that he somehow makes fit around the table. Alex drops his tray on the table and sits down next to me as if it's something he does every day.

"The nachos were a good choice," Em says with a nod to his lunch tray. Alex wouldn't have any idea that to someone not in our little circle, that was *a lot* for Em to say and he should feel special.

"That's a relief." Alex grins, and I can feel how it's very

much in my direction. I wish he would use his special powers elsewhere. Obviously in no real world is Alex Powell flirting with Jules McAllister-Morgan, but it's so easy to forget that for whole seconds at a time. Plus I have no real experience to go by, unless you count Pete Jablowski, who kissed me two summers ago at gifted camp and then ran away.

(I actually do count that.)

"Where did you move from?" Sadie asks. "Was it somewhere colder?"

"Ann Arbor, Michigan, most recently," he says. "So, yes."

"Why did you move?" she asks.

"My dad's job," he says. "It happens a lot."

"Oh, I'm Sadie," she says. "This is Justin, Thatcher, Em, and of course you know Jules."

I know to Alex it must look like I'm part of—well, not a *popular* crowd, but at least a cool one. Everyone could fill their own square in some sort of person bingo. Em's in all black in the way that's not gothy but artsy and intimidating, Thatcher's glasses are orange, so everyone knows he's really comfortable with himself, Justin—who looks like the skater that he is—has a tattoo on his right bicep because his older sister is a tattoo artist, and Sadie generally exudes cool but also specifically has very violet hair as well as a tiny hoop through her nose.

It's fate that this is my crowd and that these are my friends. Sadie's parents and my parents are best friends, and have been since before we were born. We were destined to be best friends, which is why our lunch table most certainly looks like A Lot of Cool People, plus me, wearing J.Crew.

I don't think it's ever too early to put forward a professional appearance.

Sadie's questions seem to have ended for at least the moment, which is good because I trust Sadie's good intentions but not necessarily her ability to refrain from asking about obvious topics of interests. So I'm a little relieved that Alex has a chance to eat his nachos, and also that he's not forced to confront his past as a singing and dancing dreamboat.

He looks over at me right as I think the word *dreamboat*, and I have a split second of thinking he has magical mystical mind-reading powers. "So what *are* the liaison rules?"

I'm nearly as sure that he's teasing me as that he doesn't have any psychic abilities, but I'm not positive. I force myself just to smile and not inform him of the required liaison bullet-point items and time limits. How does anyone deal with boys full-time? I'm exhausted trying just to be normal.

Talk turns to the usual subjects as people finish eating, and I stay quiet for an assortment of reasons, like Alex's presence, like that Sadie generally carries enough conversation for all of us, like my memorized multi-item list of why I'm the best choice for newspaper editor.

After the warning bell rings, Alex walks side by side with me out of the cafeteria. "I just have to take a left to get back to Maywood Hall, yeah?"

"Correct," I say, accidentally in my perfect Eagle Vista Academy Reception Committee Vice President Jules voice. Even for me, I've been a severe dork in front of Alex at this point. "I'm going that way too, actually."

I now vaguely remember from glancing at his schedule this morning that we have Topics in Economics together, and I think American literature too at the end of the day. Obviously I didn't memorize his schedule on purpose; it's just hard not remembering when you have the same classes. If I were a question-asker like Sadie, I'd get to the bottom of why Alex is hanging around with me, but I'm keeping it all locked inside. Plus he's new, and I'm an expert on the school, so it's likely incredibly obvious.

And, anyway, by the time he selects a desk near Sadie and me in American lit, the last class of the day, my brain in overdrive mode has shifted from figuring him out to my Why Jules Should Be Newspaper Editor checklist.

"Are you nervous?" Sadie asks me. I know she means to whisper, so I'm okay that other people probably hear her. "He'd be crazy not to pick you."

I glance over at Mr. Wheeler, who takes roll call every day by "studying the classroom," which means we always get at least five minutes to talk while he squints around the room figuring out attendance. "We'll see. And, yeah. I'm nervous."

She leans over and tousles my hair. We're almost exactly the same age—I'm only a month older than Sadie—but I never mind when she takes care of me. "Text me as soon as you know. We can celebrate or mourn accordingly tonight."

"I'm not sure I can," I say. "Mom and I are making meatballs, so that'll take a long time, and I have a lot of homework."

"Try," Sadie says because she seems to have stumbled upon time-bending abilities I've never been able to manage myself. If I have meatballs *and* cellular and molecular biology to worry about, I have no idea how socializing can also be slotted in. "Also save me some meatballs."

"That much I can promise!"

"What's up?" Alex asks. "Being nervous, I mean. Not the meatballs."

"They're announcing newspaper editor after school today," I say, just loudly enough for Alex and Sadie to hear me. "And it's a really big deal to me."

"She'll obviously get it," Sadie says. "Jules is a very organized genius, if you haven't noticed."

"She's already a VP," Alex says. "Editor too? Is that allowed in the constitution?"

After the last bell rings, I file out with the rest of the class, even though Mr. Wheeler's classroom doubles as the newspaper office. I like putting away my books and getting out my special red notebook and folder that I only use for this.

When people see or hear about my schedule, the automatic assumption is that I'm padding my college applications. Yes, I have newspaper, reception, and student council.

Yes, during summers I have one of those I-file-unimportant-paperwork-because-my-parent-works-here internships. Yes, I walk dogs one weekday afternoon and one weekend morning every week. But it's not only so I look good to Brown, or to any other school. All this stuff *matters*.

Okay, maybe not the filing. But everything else! And at least at the office I get to dress business-casual like I'm an adult, and the department assistant always buys me lattes when she picks up coffee orders for all the lawyers.

Alex leans against the locker next to mine. "Thanks for showing me around today. Liaison or not."

"Oh, it's just because I'm—" I cut myself off from any more liaison talk. "You're welcome."

"See you tomorrow," he says.

I think he's going to walk away, but he doesn't. "Oh! See you tomorrow too."

"Good luck with newspaper." He grins at me before heading off down the hallway. I don't know why the smile feels like the first one anyone's ever shown to me, so I focus on switching out my books and walking back into Mr. Wheeler's office.

I sit down next to Thatcher, who's already been the photography editor for the past year because he's really talented but also because he owns his own camera, and it's a *really* fancy one. Mr. Wheeler swore up and down that the camera wasn't to blame or thank for Thatcher's title, but we all suspect otherwise.

My bullet-point list is written in my red notebook, and I turn to it and reread while people file into the room. I'm only on item number four (*Showed leadership capabilities by becoming the first Reception Committee member to be elected vice president as a sophomore*) when I hear Thatcher's camera's shutter click.

I close the notebook as quickly as I can. "What are you doing?"

"When you become editor, you'll be happy that I captured a moment right before," Thatcher says. Maybe he's right, but I believe in jinxing down to my core, and hearing him say *when* makes a little shiver rock through me.

"All right, guys, let's get started," Mr. Wheeler says, walking to the front of the room. He's wearing a slouchy cardigan you'd expect to see on a very old man, not someone younger than my parents. It has elbow patches like a classic professor would have, but I feel like the slouchiness and cardiganiness take away from the academic grandeur they might otherwise suggest. "It's our first meeting of the school year, and we have a lot to accomplish."

He begins his spiel for the freshmen, who are all turning in writing, design, or photography samples today. Only some of them will make the staff, and we'll all have to drop whatever we have fourth period to take newspaper then instead.

I assume Mr. Wheeler's speech will go on awhile longer, so I sneak a peek at my list again. But I know the list by now, and I know all the reasons I can do this. And even though I can't deny Natalie deserves it probably just as much, I can't imagine my senior year writing for the *Crest* without being the editor.

Natalie always has a steel look of determination and grace, but I still want to survey her face for any hint that she's feeling what I'm feeling right now. But in glancing around the room, I realize something.

Natalie's not here.

In fact, a lot of people I expect to see aren't here. Even with the big crowd of tiny young freshman, there are a lot of empty desks.

"We always start each year with a new editor," Mr. Wheeler says, and I feel my pulse thudding in my neck and my wrists. My mouth tastes like pennies. Is it weird that I know what pennies taste like? "Every editor's been a senior who's been on board since freshman year."

Is he leading up to saying *But this year is different*, the way reality shows that have been on for ten years suddenly put contestants on teams or make men fight against women? Oh my god, I really watch too many reality shows.

"And this year's editor will be someone who's worked very hard the past three years—Jules McAllister-Morgan," he says. "Jules, would you like to say anything?"

I do have a speech, because my parents have emphasized being prepared for big life moments. But all I can say is, "What about Natalie?"

"Natalie's decided not to be on staff this year so that she can focus on other extracurriculars," Mr. Wheeler says.

"Lucky for me, huh, I don't have to make a tough decision between you two. Okay, moving on to the existing staff."

What about my speech? Mr. Wheeler couldn't really have thought it consisted of *What about Natalie?*, could he?

"All right, guys, let's talk about attendence."

I guess he could.

"Congrats," Thatcher whispers to me.

For what? I want to ask. For just not quitting? If Natalie were here, maybe I wouldn't have earned this. Maybe I didn't even earn this. Maybe I'm just the one who's sitting here. Why isn't Natalie here anyway? Why would she want to leave when this was her destiny as much as it was mine?

Mr. Wheeler discusses attendance and hands out some forms, and then I realize he's staring at me. I dismiss it for a second because unfortunately Mr. Wheeler and I know each other pretty well. He rents the guesthouse in the backyard behind ours, and for some reason my parents have befriended him. Sometimes they give him our leftovers like he'd starve without us. Isn't he a grown-up with a job, and can't grown-ups with jobs feed themselves?

"Handing over the reins to you, Jules," Mr. Wheeler says, and it hits me that even though I only got the job because Natalie's whereabouts are unknown, I still have to do the job. So I get up and take story and photo ideas.

I thought it would feel exciting and powerful, but it just feels like writing things down on the whiteboard. I feel like myself.

After class, Thatcher and I hang back with Carlos Esquivel, the layout editor. I expect Mr. Wheeler will say something big and inspirational and then maybe I'll stop feeling so blah about all of this. Mr. Wheeler, do you *want* me to feel uninspired?

"Good work, guys! See you tomorrow."

I guess he does.

CHAPTER THREE

Mom's already at home when I get there, but both dogs fling themselves at me like they've been without human interaction for decades. Since I know I'm probably too old to fling myself at Mom with the same panic-slash-relief, I sit down on the floor of the front room and focus on petting Peanut and Daisy.

Mom walks into the room with her hands behind her back, which is strange and suspicious. "Hey, how'd it go?" she asks.

"Um, it was okay." I shrug like this year's goals and dreams don't all feel like a letdown. "What are you hiding?"

Mom presents a cupcake to me with a little flourish of her hands. I wonder if I missed a memo that the fate of a school newspaper decision can only be managed via cupcakes.

"Thanks," I say because it's not her fault Sadie's cupcake arrived first. "I'm editor."

"Oh my god, Jules! Congratulations!"

"It doesn't mean anything." I stand up quickly because

Peanut has his eyes on my cupcake. I wouldn't share it with a dog anyway, but I can tell from the candy disc decoration that it's from Sprinkles, and they do have the best cupcakes in all of LA. "Natalie quit the paper or something. So Mr. Wheeler basically said I got it because he didn't have to pick."

"Aw, I can't believe he would say it like that," Mom says, because, again, *my parents adore Mr. Wheeler.* "And of course it means something."

"It doesn't feel like anything," I say. "I didn't even get to make a speech."

"You can make your speech for us."

I choose to suggest starting on the meatballs instead of giving my slaved-over speech to my mom and two dogs.

Daisy and Peanut trail us as we walk into the kitchen, and as Mom's getting everything out of the refrigerator, I think to grab my phone. I have a bunch of texts. Sadie wants to know how it went, Em knows how it went because of Thatcher and is congratulating me, and then Sadie—

Well, then Sadie has sent a second message containing something completely crazy, and I do not want to deal with that right now.

"I went to McCall's for the meat," Mom tells me as she's taking ingredients out of the refrigerator. "So it is *very* freshly ground."

"That's exciting," I say, because to Mom it is, and on a good day I guess it would be for me too. But I can't get my mind off something, and now, thanks to Sadie, it isn't the sadness of the way I became editor.

So can we talk about the fact that Alex freaking Powell is clearly into you?

Okay, I can't just *not think* about the fact that Sadie's texted me this bit of insanity.

"Is Darcy going to be home on time tonight?" I ask, even though I don't know why *on time* is something I say. It's as normal for Darcy to rush in at the tail end of the meal, calling out apologies as she throws a plate of leftovers in the microwave as it is for her to be here before I set the table. But Mom doesn't usually plan anything too elaborate unless she's pretty sure it'll be one of those latter nights and not the former.

When I was little, I didn't think there was anything strange about having two moms. And, anyway, I never really thought I had two moms. I had Mom, and I had Darcy, and they were as individual as any mom and dad were from each other. Back then we had Rochester, a beagle-shepherd mix, and we lived in our cozy house in Eagle Rock, and until I went off to kindergarten it had never really occurred to me that my family wasn't like most. Yeah, Sadie had a mom and a dad, but back then odds were to me that she was the weird one.

"Supposedly, yes. We'll see." Mom stops dumping meats into the mixing bowl and steps closer to touch my face. I hope she hasn't touched the raw meats yet. "Jules, it still means something that you were chosen to be editor."

I open my mouth to explain that my current look of weirdness and confusion isn't about the *Crest* but Sadie's insane text. In fact, it might even be to overcompensate for how just the *idea* of Alex makes me start to smile. Of course—despite what Sadie's messaging—it means nothing! And so the very last thing I want to do right now is explain to Mom why a former boy-band member definitively is *not* into me. So I just shrug and let her believe I'm upset about the thing I was—to be fair—upset about only sixty seconds ago.

"I know, Mom." I try with all my faking ability to look like I mean it too. I'm not sure if she believes me, but I manage to weasel out of this sentimental moment and pick up the recipe card.

The meatballs recipe is written out in the perfect script of my great-grandmother, who died before I was born. For the most part my family eats like normal LA people. We get our kale at the weekly farmers' market, have Meatless Mondays because it's healthy and also helps the environment, and go out for sushi at least twice a month (usually more). But Mom's the only one in her family who wanted the recipe box when her grandmother died, and once a week we cook something from it with only a few twenty-first-century changes.

My phone dings with a new text, and once I see that it's Sadie again, I don't even read the message before turning the phone facedown on the counter.

"It's a big day for you," Mom says. "Go call your friends, and I can finish this."

"It's not a big day, and I don't want to call my friends. Can't I just make meatballs in peace?"

"Of course."

Mom and I split up the rest of the ingredients. She measures out and adds ricotta, milk, and Parmesan, while I do the same with bread crumbs, basil, parsley, and salt. We split the eggs because it's our dumb tradition to see who can break them fastest. Mom wins tonight. One of my favorite things about cooking is—egg-breaking contests or not—how calming it can be. Dinner will be full of conversation, but this part isn't.

Though tonight the silence isn't doing it for me. Not with Sadie's text flashing constantly in my head.

"It's just that this new guy started today, and I was his liaison, and so he was talking to me a lot because of that, and Sadie thinks it means something."

I don't mean to say it, but I'm not that surprised I do. I've never been skilled at keeping much from my parents, but normally there isn't much to keep.

"Maybe it does mean something," Mom says.

"Sadie's crazy, and you know that."

Mom laughs because she's too nice to actually agree about Sadie's sanity levels.

"A boy could like you," Mom says, and I feel my face getting hot, which means my face is getting red. Stop it, face! Work with me, not against me. "Would that be awful?"

"No, Mom, the point is it wouldn't be possible." I feel like I'm getting too worked up, so I focus on mixing everything. You have to do it with your hands to get the best results, which is a little gross, but Mom did it last time, so it's my turn.

"You're pretty great," Mom says.

"Great to your mom is not like being great to a guy," I say. "And, anyway, I don't have time for guys. You know that."

"I know that? I know nothing of the sort!"

"I'm getting into Brown," I say. "I have to."

"You *want* to," Mom says. "You know you can't control your own destiny."

Mom says things like this all the time, but I think she believes way too much in things like *destiny*. I'm pretty sure you can make anything happen if you work hard enough, and I'm positive Darcy agrees with me. Darcy aced law school, passed the bar exam on her first attempt, and takes work home with her not because she has to, but because she wants to. It isn't that I don't think that both of my parents work hard, but Mom might sometimes hint that it would be good to take a break and go outside or to hang out at Sadie's, but I know that Darcy always understands that I don't have time for breaks.

"Boys are actually pretty easy to fit in a schedule," Mom continues. "When I was in high school—"

"Mom. I don't want to hear about fitting in boys. I shouldn't have brought this up at all. I really just want to make meat-balls, okay?"

Mom mimes zipping her lips before getting the pan ready on the stove. Now that everything's mixed, we roll the meatballs and put them into the oven. Then I fill a pot with tomato sauce we canned last summer with tomatoes from our garden. As I'm pulling vegetables out of the refrigerator to make a salad, the front door opens and Darcy walks in carrying a bakery box from the Alcove.

"Congratulations," she says before presenting the box to me. I can feel it coming, but I still look inside. More cupcakes! *Four* cupcakes! Darcy barely even believes in processed sugar, but here they are, staring at me.

"We're so proud of you," Mom says, taking a break from meatball business and walking over from the counter to stand next to Darcy. Then they just *stare at me* in the glowing way they do sometimes, and I'm not sure what to do, so I just take the box from Darcy and stand there.

"It was a technicality," I say to Darcy. "Did Mom explain that?"

Darcy frowns. "What do you mean?"

I repeat the information for her, and I wait for her face to reflect what's in my heart. But before long she's back to glowing again.

"It's not a technicality," she says. "Be proud of yourself."

Be proud of yourself sounds nice, but not necessarily when Darcy commands it.

Darcy takes over for me on salad duty, and I decide to check my phone. Sadie has messaged me twice more: I'm serious about Alex you know!! with a kissy-face emoji I've never seen before, and WHY ARE YOU IGNORING ME??? I'm coming over! I'm worried!

"Oh no," I say aloud. "I'm afraid Sadie might be coming over."

"That's great," Mom says.

"She can have the fourth cupcake," Darcy says. "I was going to give it to Joe otherwise."

I don't want Sadie interrupting my evening, but it's a much better prospect than walking a lone cupcake over to Mr. Wheeler's and pretending like we don't hear his gloomy indie rock mourning over the speakers.

The doorbell rings while we're taking the broccoli off the stove, and the meatballs are nearly ready. I'm currently managing the broccoli, so Mom lets Sadie in.

"Oh my god, it smells amazing in here," Sadie says as she walks into the kitchen. "Do you know what my family is having for dinner tonight? Turkey sandwiches. Sandwiches! A sandwich can't be dinner!"

"Your mother makes very good sandwiches," Darcy tells her. "You'll find no sympathy here."

Sadie opens the utensil drawer and starts pulling out forks, spoons, and knives to set the table. "Soooo...how did it go? Can we talk about it?"

I open my mouth to speak, but I'm still figuring out the first word when of course I don't have to.

"She got it," Mom says. "Not that any of us should be surprised."

32

"Not at all!" Sadie flings the silverware onto the table and throws her arms around me. "Yay! You did it! I told you you'd get it over Natalie."

"I didn't, okay? Can we just all acknowledge that?" I explain for the billionth time. Why doesn't anyone understand the full scope of the situation like I do?

♥ ♥ ♥

After dinner, Sadie and I walk up to my room. Peanut and Daisy follow and take their favorite spots on my bed before we can sit down. I accept where I fall on the chain of command compared to dogs in this house.

"I seriously don't want to talk any more about it," I say. "It's all been sullied."

"Seriously, Jules, I didn't come up here to talk about the paper. Wait, did you just say *sullied*?" She laughs and leans over to use Daisy as a pillow. "Alex Powell. Alex. Freaking. Powell."

"No," I say, and it sounds wimpy, so I keep going. "No no no no nooooo."

That may have somehow sounded wimpier.

"Jules. I know some things about boys. Not everything, but enough, and that is how boys act, trust me."

I manage to fit into the space between Daisy and Peanut. "What are you even saying? What is how boys act?"

"Jules, you're ranked first in our class. You'll be our valedictorian and make a lovely and wise speech we'll all remember throughout our whole lives. So don't play dumb all of a sudden."

"I'm not playing!" I run my hand over Peanut's soft tan fur. "I don't want to talk about this either. I know he acted nice. I also know it doesn't mean anything. And acting like it does feels...like I'm cheating, or something. Boys like Alex Powell don't..."

"To be fair we don't have that much reference material on boys like Alex Powell," Sadie says. "If I drop it, can I at least reserve the right to say *I told you so* later?"

"If it makes you stop talking? Yes."

"I'll take that as a victory."

CHAPTER FOUR

Natalie and I walk into cellular and molecular biology at the same time the next day, and while ignoring each other is pretty much how we normally work, I'm not sure I can today.

"Hi," I say.

"Congratulations, Julia," she says, even though *who calls me that?* "I hear Mr. Wheeler made you editor."

I still have the impulse to explain the whole technicality thing to her. But she's the very last person who requires that explanation. "Yeah."

She walks past me and takes her seat. I try not to frown at how unilluminated I am over this situation, but considering how bad I am at controlling my face, I'm sure I frown.

♥ ♥ ♥

After fourth period, I stop off at my locker to put away my newspaper stuff on my way to the cafeteria. I do consider keeping my red notebook with me to take some notes. Our table isn't exactly quiet, but I've found it's pretty easy to let the couples self-maintain and therefore get work done.

"Hey, Jules." Alex walks right up to me. "Big liaison business today?"

"No liaison business at all today," I say. "We only have meetings the first Monday of each month. Are you finding your way around all right? If you have any questions, any liaison or I could—"

"I'm actually doing fine," he says. Last night Sadie and I pulled up all the official Chaos 4 All music videos we could find on VidLook (there were only four, and three of those we'd never seen before). I feel a sense of guilt that we watched all of them (some of them up to six times), but they are just there out in the world for anyone to view.

Also, right now, we're just here out in the world—out in the hallways of Eagle Vista Academy, at least—for anyone to view. I don't think it's my imagination that everyone who walks past stares first at Alex, and then at me to figure out why he'd be talking to Jules McAllister-Morgan.

Alex reaches mere centimeters past me and taps the photo of Daisy and Peanut taped up in my locker. "Who are those?"

"Dogs," I say. "My dogs, I mean, not just, like, random dogs. Ha-ha, why would I have pictures of random dogs?"

"I don't know, they seem cool, why not? We've moved a lot, so my parents' official rule is no pets." He's so close to me right now, and it's hard not to stare at his face. I'm tall like Darcy—we're both five foot nine—but Alex is taller. His eyes are such a warm shade of brown, like if you could make a brown-colored gold. Which doesn't make sense, I know, but that's all I can think of as I look into them and—oh my god, I am standing near a boy and just flat-out looking into his eyes as if this is a thing I now do.

"Juuuuuules!" Sadie dashes up and makes a sudden stop, and I can't deny that at this very moment her suspicions or opinions about Alex Powell and his feelings toward me seem at least partially accurate. But I'm not upset she's here because this is the closest I've ever stood to a boy doing absolutely nothing, and I don't know what would even happen next if we spend more time alone in this hallway.

"Hey, Sadie," Alex says.

"Hi, Alex. Are you guys coming to lunch?"

I leave my red notebook in my locker and slam it shut. "Where else would we be going?"

"Anyone could be going anywhere," she says, walking ahead of us en route to the cafeteria. "Life's open like that."

"Don't worry," I say to Alex. "She says things like that all the time."

"I definitely wasn't worried."

I still don't know what to do. I just keep walking. Luckily once we're in the cafeteria, he wants nachos again, and I'm getting my usual salad, so I have a chance to make a break from him. Sadie joins me, even though I'm pretty sure she's not getting a salad.

"Jules."

"I don't know, okay? I don't. That's all I can say."

"That's very little."

I don't ask how Sadie figured things out with Justin, because Justin isn't her first boyfriend, and also Sadie would never need help figuring things out with people. Sadie *is* people. I know I'm a person, but somehow it's not the same.

"Ugh, look how close I almost got to getting a salad!" Sadie ruffles my hair before dashing over to butt into line with Alex.

I try to focus on getting the perfect blend of greens and protein, but it's hard to keep my mind on salad when Alex exists. When I run it over in my head, it seems ridiculous—it felt like *a moment*, but also we were literally looking at a photo of my dogs. How many romantic moments are built around looking at pictures of dogs?

And, fine, maybe it was a moment. It doesn't change the other stuff, like that Alex Powell has been *famous*, kind of. And even if that weren't true, I still don't have time for any of this. I should have definitely brought my red notebook, but one moment with a dog photo and suddenly I've turned completely irresponsible.

"Hey. *Hey.*"

I look over to my right to see a girl glaring at me, and a whole line of people behind her.

"Um, are you gonna look at garbanzo beans all day or are you gonna keep walking?"

"Sorry," I say. "They're full of protein and fiber."

There are now a lot of glaring faces in the salad line, so I forgo any bean decisions and proceed immediately to the safety of the dressing bar.

Everyone else is at the table by the time I get there, so I slide into the remaining seat between Sadie and Alex. Sadie's in the midst of polling everyone about what they think the worst soda is. Since I've already answered this one many times (Mountain Dew), I ignore the conversation and dig my phone out of my bag to see if Mom or Darcy has messaged about anything. I drive straight from school to where I volunteer on Wednesday nights, so sometimes texting is the only way we can coordinate dinner.

I do have a new message, and from only one minute ago. But it's not from either one of my parents. It's from a 734 number I don't know.

What are you doing tonight?

I tell myself not to look over at Alex. But I look over at Alex. He pauses from nacho-eating and grins at me. I don't know what to do with all the grinning.

I stare back at the phone and type my answer with shaky hands.

I volunteer at Stray Rescue on Wednesdays.

Alex doesn't have his sound off on his phone—breaking a pretty major school rule! Should I have gone over cell phone procedures in the liaison introduction yesterday? Whatever, the point is that Alex's phone audibly receives a text, and everyone looks over, or at least it feels like everyone. It's actually just Sadie and Em.

But Alex just picks up his phone and starts typing back. Sadie smiles right at me, so I look away. My heart pounds in my neck, which is a weird place for my heart to suddenly be. And I realize I am not in the mood for my salad. And it's not the salad's fault; everyone's food looks awful.

My phone buzzes again. I try not to look down immediately, but Sadie's still watching me, so the speed of my looking down won't really make me more or less suspicious.

I could come with you, if they need more volunteers.

Another message comes in while I'm holding the phone.

Wait, is it dogs? Dogs are cool. If it's wildlife I don't know.

"Of course it's dogs," I say, and then I remember we aren't having this conversation aloud. We're having it on our phones.

"What's dogs?" Sadie asks. "Who are you guys texting?"

"No one and nothing," I say. "I mean, nothing and no one."

I look back to my phone, even though I can feel everyone staring at me.

Why would it be wildlife? No one calls wildlife strays! I just walk dogs for a few hours. It's really easy, if you actually want to come.

Did I just ask a boy out? No, I just asked *Alex Powell* out. I don't even have any normal-boy experience, and here I am, jumping straight into Former Teen Idol territory. What am I doing?

"I'm not hungry." I jump up and shove my phone into my purse. I start to take my salad with me to throw away, but I immediately think about how many people around the world and even in this very city are hungry. "Someone can have this salad if they want it. You guys know I don't believe in throwing away food."

Once I'm out of the cafeteria, I don't know where to go, and I'm still wavering between the bathroom and the library when someone steps up next to me.

"I like it when you freak out," Sadie says. "I wish it happened more."

"What is even going on?" I ask.

"Uh, something super exciting? I *like* him, Jules. Not like that, just—he's cute and funny and tall and seems smart. All very good boy qualities."

"No one's ever liked me," I say.

"I'm sure that's not true," Sadie says.

"You sound like my mom."

"Which one? Wait, who cares! They're both great."

"I don't know what to do," I say. "It doesn't feel real."

"It never feels real when it's good," she says. "The first time I kissed Justin, we might as well have been in outer space."

"Outer space is real," I say.

"Jules! You're missing the point."

"We're not supposed to be in the hallway."

Sadie grabs my arm and yanks me into the bathroom. She checks under all the stall doors before hopping up to sit on the row of sinks. "He asked me for your number. He's texting you. These are all real signs—no, not signs. Stuff is *happening*."

"I don't know what to do," I say again.

"There's no specific thing to do."

"There's always a specific thing to do." I get out my phone again. Alex has sent another text:

I can walk dogs!

"Okay, well, the specific thing to do is just see what happens. That's it."

"That's not very specific." I glance in the mirror as if maybe I've forgotten to for a while and maybe I've gotten a lot hotter and this will all make sense. But I look the way I always look.

"Are there steps?" I ask. "You could write down steps for me."

"Oh my god, Jules, you weirdo. Boys aren't like your college application checklist. Boys are people, and we're people and, come on, you have friends! You know how to act with people. You're fine."

My phone buzzes again.

You ok?

"He's so nice," I say. "Or at least he acts nice. I don't get it."

"Just enjoy it. Period. End of sentence. Last advice."

"Oh, I doubt that."

We both laugh, and I take a moment to text back to Alex that I am okay. I'm not sure it's accurate, but it feels like the right response.

"I'm going to finish my lunch," Sadie says, fluffing her hair in the mirror. "Come with?"

"I'm going to the library to work on a few things." I follow her into the hallway and gesture in the opposite direction down the hallway. "But see you in English."

"See you then." She starts to head off, but nearly immediately turns around. "Wait. Can I seriously eat your salad?"

♥ ♥ ♥

Mr. Wheeler finds me when I'm leaving the library after lunch, and he gives me the freshman submissions. I decide that even though I have time, I probably shouldn't actually seek out Alex right now. What am I going to tell him...the truth? There's no way any other girl that Alex went out with or whatever didn't understand how to proceed with just *the concept* of dating *or whatever* so I should probably keep as much to myself as I can. That's easy to do in economics because Ms. Schmidt starts talking the second the bell rings and doesn't let up until the next one sounds. But Alex sits by me, and as soon as we're dismissed he's just right there.

"I'm in for the dogs," he says. "But I have to admit something to you that could totally change how you see me."

"Oh," I say as I'm instantly sweaty and fighting a blush—that is, *actually blushing.* "Yeah? Uh-huh? Yes?"

I cut myself off before I keep going, but everything's pounding as I wait for Alex to reveal his boy-band past or however he's going to explain it to me. I wonder if I can fake an expression of surprise.

"I don't know how to drive," he says. "So you'll have to take me."

"Oh," I say again, and I wish I could see my face because then I could use it for reference when I am faking surprise for real. "That's not a big deal. I don't mind."

When we step out of Ms. Schmidt's classroom, my face must be reflecting even more surprise, because there are bright blue flyers everywhere. TALON IS COMING, they say, with a little icon of an eagle.

"This is very strange." I mean to just think it, and the way it comes out of my mouth sounds way more full of wonder than the average person would be at seeing some flyers. "It's just that there are very strict rules with administration about what's allowed to be hung in hallways. It's supposed to only be from officially recognized school groups."

Alex grins at me. "Then I guess someone from an officially recognized school group did them."

I know he's teasing me, but at least he's teasing me. And I'm definitely blushing when I head off to calculus, so maybe I'll have to start getting used to this as my new state of being.

I still think Sadie could provide me with a checklist, though, if she really wanted.

CHAPTER FIVE

Everyone in calculus and then in American lit is talking about the flyers, because at least in my classes this is the kind of event that rates extreme gossip levels. Either no one knows what TALON is or no one who knows is willing to say, because speculation is all that happens. ("A gang?" "A cult?" "A dance battle group?" These are all serious guesses by people whose grades are good enough to be in AP courses.)

But I barely participate in any speculation, because time is ticking down until I'll be walking dogs with Alex Powell. On paper it would sound ridiculous, but I reread the texts at least seven times, and it's really going to happen.

Alex and Sadie walk out of American lit with me, but Sadie somehow quickly disappears, and then it's just Alex and me.

Already!

"I'll meet you at your locker," Alex says, and then he's gone too. It's much easier to figure out which books I need to take home without Alex's company, but they're barely in my bag before he's back at my side.

"You don't have to go if you don't want to," I tell him, even though now I can't imagine walking dogs without Alex. Is it even possible? "In case you offered to be nice."

"I never do anything to be nice," he says in a voice that sounds extra deep. And then it's like earlier, when all of a sudden he's close. The moment becomes A Moment. His eyes are like metal and mine magnets, or maybe it's the other way around, but it doesn't matter because there's no possibility I could pull away. When you think about it, you can spend your whole life around people and yet never hold someone's gaze with your own.

Actually, it feels more like my gaze is being held.

"We should go," I say, because I don't know where to take this. Or I guess I have an idea, but I can't imagine kissing him on school property. I can't imagine kissing him at all. So I lead him outside to my car. He climbs into the passenger side and his tall frame just kind of melts into the seat. I feel my brain again head down the path of attempting to calculate how any of this is happening to me, but then I realize something.

I can tell my brain to shut up.

I drive down Eagle Rock Boulevard to York Boulevard, which is definitely one of the cooler parts of LA. There are vintage boutiques, coffee shops, hipster bars, a Manic Panic salon where Sadie sometimes gets her hair dyed, and a dough-nut shop I let myself stop in only after I've walked many dogs around many blocks. I point it all out to Alex as we make our way to Highland Park Stray Rescue, and he looks at everything with attention, especially Donut Friend.

I find parking directly behind the rescue, and I show Alex in. Tricia, who usually works the front desk, grins at me and waves as we walk inside.

"Happy Wednesday, Jules! How was school?"

"It was pretty good. This is my... this is Alex. He wanted to help out today. That's okay, right?"

"Of course." She leans over the desk to shake his hand. "You're so tall!"

"Thanks?" Alex smiles at her. "And thanks for letting me help out."

"Of course. Once you fill out this form, you can follow Jules to see where to pick up the dogs and where to walk them. Since it's your first time, you should only take dogs with green collars. That means they don't have any behavioral issues and won't act up on leash. Sound good?"

"What color collars are you allowed to walk?" he asks me.

"Any of them," I say. "But I've had a lot of experience now. I've been volunteering since we got Daisy two years ago."

I wait for Alex to complete the volunteer form, and then lead him down a row of kennels. The dogs on both sides bark as we make our way down, and of course those barks set off a chorus of barks throughout the building. Santiago, the afternoon and evening coordinator, is settling a German shepherd mix back after a walk, but he waves as soon as he's able.

"It's Jules day! And Lola's walk is up next."

"Lola!" I lean down to smile at Lola, a bouncy border collie and black lab mix, who I've been walking for at least a month now. I hate that she hasn't found a home yet—she's seven, and a lot of people want puppies or at least younger dogs—but I'm always glad to see her again.

Santiago looks from the German shepherd to Alex. "Hey, thanks for coming. I'm Santiago."

Alex reaches over to shake Santiago's hand, and I feel my stomach flip-flop over how grown up he looks. This isn't how boys shake hands; these are men.

"You look familiar," Santiago says, and my glow over Alex's handshaking ability is gone. I hold my breath and hope that the words *Chaos*, *4*, and *All* won't be uttered.

"I've got one of those faces," Alex says with a grin.

"So, Jules, this your boyfriend?"

I move quickly to correct this statement. "Alex is—" *WHACK*.

I somehow just slammed my face into the front of Lola's kennel. Slamming your face into a metal grid will make your eyes water like you're crying—probably even if you aren't suffering total humiliation about the assumed relationship status of the boy you've brought with you. But since I am, now I'm dealing with not just the humiliation but the tears as well.

"Are you okay?" Santiago and Alex both ask, and I'm pretty sure I'm fine, but my eyes won't stop watering. Lola lets out a little yip of concern, and then other dogs start barking, and the barking echoes out in concentric circles from my epicenter of humiliation.

"I'm fine," I finally say, and I'm not sure whether it's seconds or minutes or hours later. "I'm ready to take out Lola. I'm fine."

I reach in to connect a leash to Lola's collar and realize that since the rule is dogs have to be taken outside immediately once they're on a leash, I can't clear up any boyfriend misconceptions or explain the usual walking route to Alex or make sure he's matched with a fun but easy dog. I just hustle Lola out of the building and down Avenue 52.

Lola looks back at me while we're walking, and I'm pretty sure she's just panting, but it looks like a comforting smile. I smile back. Then she pees on a patch of grass, so it feels less like we're having a bonding moment.

Eventually I hear Alex and Santiago, and I glance back to see they're walking in tandem with green-collared dogs. When Alex and I were riding down York with the sun shining, I didn't expect that his dog-bonding experience would be with Santiago. But I make my way around with Lola, and then it's time for Hudson, and Noodle, and Keno. I keep walking dogs, and I keep trying to delete from my brain that Santiago referred to Alex as my boyfriend.

I manage the first thing. The second, not at all.

Our volunteer shift is over at five, and I say good night to the staff and wait for Alex to catch up. I watch as he thanks Santiago and Tricia, and I try to identify the feeling washing over me. I think I might be proud of Alex for being so good with everyone, and maybe I'm proud of myself for bringing him here.

"I'm pretty sure I was promised doughnuts," he says, so I lead him down the block to Donut Friend. I get a traditional doughnut with lemon glaze, but Alex—after spending at least five minutes reading the menu—goes all out with a doughnut cut bagel-style and stuffed with peanut butter and jelly. We take seats along the counter lining the back wall, and I try to determine if there's an especially delicate way to eat a doughnut.

"Hey, so, I'm gonna tell you something," Alex says at the exact same moment I decide to bite into the doughnut. I still try to look like I'm ready to hear anything he wants to tell me, but all at once I realize there are so many things he might have to tell me that I'm actually not ready for. What if he has a girlfriend at his old school? What if he wants to clarify exactly how much he does not like me? What if I found exactly the least delicate way to eat a doughnut ever, and it's so bad he has to tell me?

That last one probably isn't true, but now I can't put it out of my head. Doughnuts don't seem romantic! Why did I pick doughnuts? Why does my whole week feel defined by pastries?

"A few years ago, I was really into singing and dancing, and one thing just led to another, and…honestly, I ended up in this boy band." He shrugs with one eyebrow cocked, and I don't know him well enough to figure out if he's pretending to be casual or he's just casual. "We had one really big hit—not to sound like an ass, but you definitely heard it at some point—but we ended up being kind of a one-hit wonder. So that was that."

"Wow," I say, and I widen my eyes so that I look legitimately shocked. "That's...legitimately shocking."

He laughs. "It barely feels like it actually happened to me. Like it was some weird movie I saw at one point."

I nod and raise my eyebrows a little like I'm surprised by every new tidbit of information.

"And that's it."

"Okay," I say, and then I decide I'm not saying enough, but I don't know what else to say. I just stare at him, and that feels worse than not speaking. He has to know I don't care about this revelation, but maybe the staring and muteness is giving the opposite impression.

"I'll tell you something too, not that it's a secret. And not that it's a big deal. I mean, not that your boy-band thing is a big deal, just...never mind about that, sorry. I just thought I'd tell you that I have two moms."

"Oh, cool," he says, then makes a face. "Not 'cool,' no, not that it's uncool, just, yeah, sure, that isn't a big deal, no—shit, I feel like I'm saying everything wrong."

"Me too," I say, and we both laugh, and it's like out of nowhere I can see how people end up falling in love with each other. Oh my god, not that I'm in love with Alex. Just that if within the span of days you can feel so honest with someone, you can see how bigger things might be possible too.

"Is it weird?" I ask. "If you don't mind...because of the boy band?"

"Sometimes," he says. "You can see...not the best side of

people. They can be so fake just because of your fame or what they think they could get from you. Or they pretend to be one way publicly, but in reality they're not a good person."

"That sounds awful," I say.

"Sometimes it is, yeah." He smiles again. "I'm done with all that bullshit. You're not like any of those people. It's really cool you care about stuff."

I look down at my nearly finished doughnut, but I'm sure Alex can still see my smile. And how red my face is.

♥ ♥ ♥

"Can you give me directions to your house?" I ask Alex once we're back in my car.

"What?" He laughs his deep and warm laugh. "I definitely cannot, but my mom wrote down my address. Hang on." He digs through his backpack before pulling out a notebook, where I see that it's carefully printed on the inside cover. "We just moved, remember. I'm not an idiot, about that at least."

"I think it's cute your mom wrote it out for you," I say, but maybe that sounds sarcastic, so I just let it go at that. I type the address into my GPS and wait for the computerized voice to guide me.

CHAPTER SIX

At school the next day I decide to stop eyeing Alex with suspicion when he pops up near me. And that's good because he keeps doing that. My locker, the hallway, the salad line in the cafeteria (though he abandons it for chicken fingers).

I can feel the eyes of the school on us. In my head they're asking *Why her? Why Jules McAllister-Morgan?* But no one says it aloud.

On Thursdays I have Associated Student Body after school, so even though Alex asks, politely, for a ride home while leaning against the locker next to mine, I have to turn him down.

"Let's get this shitshow over with," Em greets me as I walk up to the conference room in the administrative building. She's our class treasurer, and I'm the recording secretary. That would bother me, except that Natalie's neither the president nor the vice president but the public relations director. This is the one extracurricular that's more of a popularity contest than an earned honor, so we picked roles we actually had a shot at. Em admitted she's only padding her college applications, and considering that ASB hasn't actually changed anything about the school in the past three years, maybe that's what we're all doing.

"So do you want to talk about it?" Em whispers. Hers, the opposite of Sadie's, is a real whisper.

I gesture to my phone, recording the meeting so I can verify my minutes before submitting them to Ms. Reinhardt, our faculty advisor, and then go back to taking notes. Em writes furiously in her notebook, which is odd because she's the treasurer, so she's not responsible for capturing every moment like I am.

She shoves the notebook in my direction. *so do you want to talk about it??* It's next to a realistic sketch of an avocado.

What does the avocado symbolize? I write below, even though I normally try harder to resist Em's attempts to distract me during meetings.

oh god jules. i'm bored and doodling. sometimes an avocado is just an avocado. Then she snatches the notebook back from me and scribbles for a few moments. Now the avocado has dark wavy hair like Alex's as well as his eyebrows. A giggle bursts out of me like a hiccup, and then Em snorts. Since there are only twenty people plus Ms. Reinhardt here, everyone hears us.

"Is there something you want to share with the whole class, Miss Han or Miss McAllister-Morgan?" Michael Alves asks in a perfect impression of Teacher Voice. As senior class president, he's in the midst of his student address, so it seems fair that he's making fun of us. Though, for a person cool enough to win the populist vote ASB presidency requires, it's in a pretty dorky fashion.

"Sorry," I say.

"Carry on," Em adds, which unfortunately causes another laugh to squeak out of me. I've been on ASB every year since sixth grade, but I never had to make an effort to behave until Em joined during junior year. Before then I didn't even realize I was corruptible.

♥ ♥ ♥

Alex texts while I'm reading through the freshman submissions for the *Crest* when I'm at home later. If it were anyone else, I'd probably make it through the whole stack and at least start on my final list for Mr. Wheeler before reading it.

But it's an understatement to say Alex isn't anyone else.

Want to hang out Saturday?

Of course I want to hang out Saturday. But hanging out Saturday would be a date, maybe? It's definitely not on my list of activities I'd planned on participating in my senior year. But it's *Alex*.

And to be technical about it, he didn't say *go out*, he said *hang out*. And that sounds less nerve-wracking, somehow.

I neatly stack the papers on my bed and type back to Alex.

I walk dogs in the morning. After that I'm free.

I go back to reading even though I feel I'm not being as fair to the freshmen as I could be. I'm of course evaluating their style, grammar, choice of topic, original voice. But I'm also wondering how Alex will respond. I'm wondering what hanging out will entail. I'm wondering if it's too soon to kiss him. I'm wondering if he'll be the one to make that happen, because I'm not sure I'll have the nerve. Somewhere in the back of my mind—in all honesty it's probably closer to the front of my mind—I'm not sure I have the right to make that call.

He's Alex Powell. And I'm just me.

I start texting all of this to Sadie, but it's turning into less of a message and more of an essay, so I delete it and get out my laptop to email her. Even this looks longer than could be typically constrained by email, but I hit send and then text her to make sure she'll check it.

My phone buzzes less than a full sixty seconds later.

"You couldn't possibly have read all of that," I answer.

"Of course I didn't! I hit the stupid point, and I had to call you immediately," Sadie says, and I actually feel myself gasp because I'm not sure Sadie has ever called me stupid.

"He's him and you're *you*?" she asks. "Oh my god, Jules. Jules! Yes, he used to be famous, but you're *amazing.*"

"Of course you think that!" I say. "You have to."

"I don't have to! Who's making me?"

"Society," I said. "Best friend rules."

"Oh, shut up." Sadie laughs. "Alex likes that you're overachieving."

"How do you know? Maybe he's just humoring me. Maybe he's just doing something where he conquers girls one by one at a new school." I hadn't even thought of these possibilities until they were out of my mouth, but now I'm terrified they're true.

"I know because I'm not blind. Some people make what they're feeling really obvious, and that, my friend, is Alex Powell. Also I guess we can talk about the obvious stuff, like that you're cute and your hair is pretty and you pull off that whole preppy thing really well."

"I still think that you have to think that," I say.

"Oh yes, the international best friend bylaws, sure. Since when have you seen me obey any rules I think are stupid? Since *never*, Jules."

Sadie had me there.

♥ ♥ ♥

Friday night is the third year of our first-week-of-school tradition, which involves meeting up at Casa Bianca. It's a small traditional Italian restaurant with the best pizza maybe on not just the Eastside but all of LA. By dinnertime there can be a line to get a table, but since we're out of school at three we decide to be there when the door opens at four.

"We can't do this next year," I say as we're seated at a booth in the front dining room. "We'll be living in different cities."

"Sadie and I won't," Em says. "Remember? We'll be in the same city, just different schools. We can get pizza on our first Friday."

"Cheap and greasy delicious New York pizza!" Sadie closes her eyes as if just the thought is too beautiful for her.

I've lived in the same house my whole life, and Sadie has lived in the same house her whole life, and those houses are only a ten-minute drive apart. I'm not sure what life will be like with her in Manhattan and me in Rhode Island. I'm excited about college and I'm excited about my future, but only recently did I start thinking about how all of that means my present has to end. Next year it won't be the three of us, and I guess that means it won't really be the three of us ever again after this school year.

"Why do you look depressed, Jules?" Em asks.

"Ugh, I have to work on my face not showing everything," I say instead of answering. But, I do.

"You have no future in poker," Em says. "But I would be surprised to hear you were even considering a future in poker."

"So what's up with Alex?" Sadie asks. "That's not why you look depressed, is it?"

"It's not why I look depressed," I say. "I know Alex acts like he likes me."

Today had been another day of that. Alex at my locker, Alex asking questions, Alex grinning at me when the mood didn't call for anything more than *neutral*. Alex, Alex, Alex. My whole year was supposed to be about the *Crest*, the Reception Committee, college applications.

I don't know what it's supposed to be about now.

"But?" Em raises an eyebrow.

"Oh, I mean, no, no *but*. I just mean that I'm aware of it. We're hanging out tomorrow."

"'Hanging out!'" they chorus—even Sadie who's aware this was a possibility.

"He's coming with me to Stray Rescue," I say. "And I'm not sure what after that. Maybe that's all."

"Don't you walk dogs at like six in the morning?" Em asks.

"Eight," I say. "That's when they need the most help."

"He must like you *a lot* to get up that early just to walk dogs," Sadie says.

"Eight isn't that early. And maybe he's a morning person," I say. "Maybe he wants to do something good for the world."

"No one wants to do something good for the world before ten on a Saturday," Em says. "Except you."

♥ ♥ ♥

Darcy and Mom are hanging out in the living room watching TV when I get home. I take it as a sign to talk. Okay, actually, it's more that I have no idea how to keep any information from my parents, but I like the idea of fate.

"Soooooo," I say, and the word comes out for much longer than I mean it to. "There's this new boy in school."

Mom perks up. "The boy that Sadie thinks likes you?"

Now Darcy's perked up too. "Sadie thinks a boy likes Jules?"

"Look how *red* you are," Mom says.

"Don't tease her," Darcy says, but they're both giggling.

"I didn't say this the other day, but...he was in Chaos 4 All. If you remember that video."

"If we *remember*?" Darcy hums, and I realize it's "Want 2 B Ur Boy."

"Don't do that," I say. "He's just like a normal guy now. He doesn't like to make a big deal about it."

"So Sadie's right?" Mom asks in her gentlest voice.

"Yes," I say, staring down at my feet, and at least this time she doesn't comment on my face's redness. She doesn't say anything at all, and neither does Darcy. I take a deep breath and look up. They're beaming at each other.

"Your first boyfriend," Mom says. "I remember my first boyfriend."

"Me too," Darcy says, because they actually went to high school together, even though it took them a lot longer to fall in love with each other. "Matt Hale. I remember he wore that AC/DC shirt all the time."

"I thought that was really sexy," Mom says, which is disturbing. Not that she went out with guys in high school and college—

that much I already knew. But no one should ever have to hear what their parents think is sexy, about anyone, ever. "Meanwhile you were dating half of the girls at St. Elizabeth's."

"*Half* is a strong word," Darcy says. "And so is *dating*."

"Can we change the subject to something less disturbing?" I ask. "Please?"

"Remember that in the music video they had different traffic signs they danced with?" Darcy asks. "I still think about that sometimes when I see yield signs."

I cover my face with my hands. Unfortunately even when I can't see them, my parents still exist. "Oh my god."

"We'll behave when we meet him," Darcy says.

"We promise!" Mom says. "When do we get to meet him?"

"I don't know. And he's not my boyfriend," I say. "But we're hanging out tomorrow. We're walking dogs together."

"After that, bring him by," Mom says. "If you want."

"No pressure!" Darcy says. "I won't sing."

"Are you friends with Matt Hale on Facebook?" Darcy asks Mom, and they start laughing about how he named all his kids after spices (with Basil being the oldest and Saffron the youngest), and I'm free to escape to my room with the dogs.

I know Peanut and Daisy don't really understand English, but I can't imagine they're up for this Matt Hale conversation either.

CHAPTER SEVEN

I pick up Alex the next morning at seven forty-five. Darcy got up and brewed coffee for us, so I filled two travel mugs and brought along two bananas from the bowl on the counter.

At least I hope that was the intent of the coffee, and Mom and Darcy aren't wondering what happened to it.

"Hey." He gets into the car and grins at me. "Thanks for picking me up."

"Thanks for going with me."

We sip our coffees in silence for a bit as I navigate over to Highland Park. Alex stares out the window, as if he's logging every tree, every shop, every street sign. This is Alex's new home, and he must want to know it.

After waving to Tricia once we're inside Stray Rescue, we head right back to find Santiago in the first row of kennels. He leashes up a bulldog for Alex, while I take a husky mix named Luna.

"You did a great job last week," Santiago tells Alex. "So you won't be stuck with me this time. I'll let your girlfriend supervise you."

Oh my god, Santiago.

"Great" is all Alex says, though.

And luckily I don't slam my face into any cages.

Outside I'm desperately rolling through my brain in the attempt to come up with anything to distract from the *girlfriend* talk.

"How's the editor gig going?" Alex asks.

"It's good, I guess. I submitted a list of the freshmen I think should be accepted to Mr. Wheeler, so that was really fun, getting to read all their ideas. I reread my old submission, since I save all my old papers, and you can tell I've definitely improved a lot in three years. It's fun thinking where these freshman might be three years from now, ability-wise."

Oh my god, *Jules.* Why do I say so much more than I'm aware a person needs to say?

"Cool," Alex says anyway as we pause while our dogs pee. "Is it a big deal to you because you want to run a newspaper someday? Uh, like a real newspaper? Not to insult this one, but, y'know. Not a high school one."

"Not a newspaper," I say. "Maybe a political campaign? Or an organization? I like working with a bunch of people to get one goal achieved. And right now, the *Crest* is kind of the best option I have. And it has this whole history; it's over a hundred years old. I like feeling part of that whole thing."

"I wish I knew what I wanted to do," he says. "I used to. Who knows now."

I'm trying to think of the right thing to say to that when the bulldog turns around and bounds right at Alex. He laughs and leans over to pet it.

"Before," he says, and pauses. "Before...no one I know would have done something like this if there wasn't a camera crew nearby to capture it. And you do it twice a week, all the time."

"A camera crew wouldn't be very interested in me," I say.

"You know what I mean," he says. Suddenly, all his attention is off the bulldog and on me. "You're not like anyone from that world."

♥ ♥ ♥

While walking a dachshund and a black lab, I ask what it was like signing autographs, and he says people mainly wanted selfies, but either way, it was weird.

While walking a pit bull and a yellow lab, he tells me that his last school had a statue of their town's founder out front, and kids have rubbed the crotch of it so much as a joke that now the crotch is a different color than the rest of it.

And while walking a miniature pinscher and a shepherd mix, I tell him how last year we made a joke issue of the *Crest* with a photo we found of Mr. Wheeler in college performing improv, and it almost accidentally got sent to the printer the week he went on vacation and the substitute advisor wasn't paying attention.

Of course after our time is up with Stray Rescue we walk to Donut Friend. Alex dives right into his Bacon 182 (yes, it's a doughnut with bacon on it—though it's technically vegan bacon made from coconut) while I let my standard traditional with lemon glaze sit there while I figure out how to ask him to continue this day.

"Um," I start, and then wish I could start over immediately. *Um* is such a dorky nervous sound to make with your mouth. "After this do you want to come over? You can meet my dogs. Also my moms. You don't have to if you don't want to. Or if you're busy. It's not a big deal."

"I want to meet your dogs and your moms," he says. "And I'm not busy."

"Okay," I say.

"How do you think people figured out bacon's good on doughnuts?" Alex asks.

"They're both breakfast foods," I say. "Maybe some bacon fell on a doughnut."

He laughs. "Ah, so Jules has an answer for everything."

"That's an obvious answer! How do *you* think bacon got on doughnuts?"

" 'Maybe some bacon *fell* on a doughnut'?" Alex laughs even harder. "Fell from where?"

"Just another part of the plate. Don't make fun of me."

Alex mimes bacon falling sideways onto my doughnut, and I wave his hands away.

"Leave my doughnut out of this," I say.

He does his eyebrow thing. I try not to be visibly affected.

"I'm just trying to prove your scientific hypothesis."

"Alex, I never said it fell *sideways*."

As we walk back to my car and I drive to my house, I keep thinking of ways I could kiss him. It's not that I in any way feel qualified to make the first move, but my lips are actually tingling. Even my lips know that maybe it's time.

Unfortunately I don't know how to break it to my lips that even when we're at a long stoplight on York, I can't lean over and kiss Alex. A force field might as well be around me.

Peanut and Daisy leap all around Alex when we walk inside, and he takes a lot of time to pet each of them, which is impressive. Peanut's so much more demanding, but Alex moves back and forth between them evenly.

"Hi," I hear, and when I look up, Mom and Darcy are both standing right there.

"Hi," I say. "This is Alex. Alex Powell. Alex, these are my moms. Mom and Darcy."

He rises to his feet in a split second and shakes their hands. "It's really nice to meet you both."

They give me a simultaneous look, like, *Good job selecting a boy who is polite to adults.* Even though it's probably not possible, I feel as if Daisy and Peanut are giving me that look too.

"How did you decide which one of you got to be called

Mom?" Alex looks back and forth between them. "If that's okay to ask."

"Of course it's okay." Darcy waves off the other possibility with her whole arm.

"We tried to think of all the mother options," Mom says. "Mom, Mother, Maman—as if we were French? I don't know. Right before Jules was born, I think we'd finally settled on Mom and Mama, except that neither one of us wanted to be Mama."

"We kept thinking, *Who'll want to say* mama *when they're an adult?*" Darcy says. "We could barely say it to each other, and we were solidly in the throes of new parenthood. So I decided if everyone else in my life who mattered just called me Darcy, why not my daughter? It felt fine."

"And then I got to be Mom!" Mom says. "Which was a huge relief by then."

"That's nice," Alex says, which from someone else might be a dismissal, but I can tell from the warmth of his voice and how he's smiling that he really thinks it is nice, as nice as I know that it is.

"Can we take the dogs into the backyard?" I ask. I don't need permission to go with my own dogs to my own backyard, but I do think they'll take the hint.

"Of course," Darcy says. "We bought a new Frisbee, if you'd like to try it out."

"Yeah," Alex says with a surge of enthusiasm. So we get the new Frisbee and an old tennis ball, and we head to the backyard. Mom and Darcy have stayed inside, and I try not to just stare at Alex. This must be it, though, the moment things really *happen*. I might be inexperienced, but I feel how my nerves seem to rise up through my skin in Alex's direction.

"We're alone," Alex says, and I stare at him, and he bursts into laughter. "I don't know why I said that like a creep."

"It's okay," I say. "I know you're not a creep."

It's as if now neither one of us knows what to do with this moment. I decide to make the moment mine. I turn a little, and even though we're not standing exactly facing each other, it seems close enough. I gently rest my hand on his side, even though I've never just reached out and touched a boy before. He feels solid and warm and so real beneath my hand. Something in his expression shifts, and while Alex is always smiling, this smile is different. This smile is new, and it's somehow focused right on me.

Peanut barks, and I manage not to yell at him. Alex grabs the Frisbee and races down the length of the backyard before throwing it in my direction. I have no idea where he's gotten the idea that I'm athletically inclined, but I do manage to catch it. The dogs leap around in glee, so I fling the plastic disc toward Alex, but not *really*, so that Peanut's able to leap up and catch it in his mouth. Alex thinks he can just take the Frisbee back from Peanut, but I don't say anything so I can watch a fifteen-pound dog and a full-grown boy battle it out.

Peanut wins, of course.

We keep playing until the dogs are lying, panting, on the

grass. I'm not sure if I can just pick up again where we were, but then Alex is right next to me.

Then we move at the same time, and though this is only my second kiss since Pete Jablowski, it doesn't matter—every cell in me knows what to do. Everything's in sync, how I have to rise up on my toes just a little, and Alex leans over the tiniest amount. My hands suddenly aren't at my sides but meeting each other around his neck. Alex's have slid around my waist, skimming lines that feel drawn onto me permanently.

And the kissing. The kissing! Our lips have parted, finding new and newer ways to overlap. He's still sugary and salty from the Bacon 182. I'm convinced we're breathing through each other, that we're all the oxygen we could possibly need.

"That was so good," I say once the kissing's ended. And then I try to figure out how to reverse time and pull those words back inside of me. "Oh my god. I'm sorry."

"Sorry why?" Alex grins down at me. His hands are still on the small of my back, and as long as he keeps making tiny little movements with his fingertips, I'm probably going to release stupider and stupider things from the depths of my brain.

"That was the dorkiest thing I could say."

"You know what I hate?" He leans down and kisses the corner of my mouth. "People who calculate everything that comes out. Who think they're supposed to be a certain way or like a certain thing, and it's all some act. I've had enough of that."

I'm afraid of what other words I might blurt out, so I lean into him and find his mouth with mine. I'm aware it's my third kiss with Alex, fourth overall, but then, so quickly, I lose count. Some of the kisses are brief, like a spark in the darkness, while some go on slow and deep and dizzying.

"Should we go in?" Alex leans his forehead against mine, so we're still close like we're kissing. My lips actually ache. "I don't want your moms to be angry."

The dogs seem to be over their temporary Frisbee-based exhaustion, so we distract ourselves by throwing the tennis ball for them before heading inside. Mom and Darcy are working on a recipe at the kitchen counter, but they pause to share a knowing look.

"We're making biscotti," Mom says.

"You two should go out for lunch," Darcy says. "We have nothing in the house."

I know for a fact that it's not true. We freeze leftovers, and we have sauces and jams preserved in the cabinet, and there is always fresh produce from the farmers' market. My parents are just encouraging me to be alone with a boy.

My parents are amazing.

Even though we could walk to lunch, if I really wanted that, now that we've kissed, I want car time with Alex. We act as we did before, but after our lunch at Taco Spot we pile back into the car and kind of right into each other. Normally, I'd be completely against public displays of affection, but I parked farther away than I needed to for this exact reason.

"You taste like nachos," I tell him, and he cracks up. We're still as close as we were when we were kissing, so I feel his laughter warm into my neck. Once, a few months ago, I was walking a dog around my normal Stray Rescue route and saw a couple kissing in their parked car. I tried imagining wanting to kiss someone so much that the public didn't matter.

And now I don't have to try.

♥ ♥ ♥

After I get home from dropping Alex off at his house, I'm planning to review all the freshman submissions for the *Crest*. But Sadie texts what I know is not an innocuous So what's up??, and I find myself typing what's practically an essay about walking dogs and eating doughnuts and meeting my parents, and I save the kissing for the very end of the story. It takes so long that Sadie sends two follow-up texts (TELL ME EVERYTHING and then You've been typing for an hour so maybe you should just CALL ME JULES) in the meanwhile. But I finish the whole thing and hit send, and then I'm holding my phone and thinking about Alex.

Is it too early to text? No, I'm pretty sure once you've kissed someone a bunch of times, you can at least text them. Thanks for walking dogs with me today! feels like a safe start, but I don't have a chance to see how long he'll take to respond, if he responds at all, because Sadie's calling.

"Oh my god, Jules," she says before I can even say hello.

"Is it surprising?" I ask. "Are you surprised?"

"After seeing how he's been looking at you for this whole week now? *No.* I just want more details."

"I texted you every detail!" I say.

"I don't care. Tell me everything again."

I can't blame Sadie. This is definitely the only non-dorky exciting thing that's ever happened to me.

"Did you feel like you were kissing in outer space?" Sadie asks after I repeat the whole story.

"Sadie, I still don't know why you think that means something romantic."

CHAPTER EIGHT

Alex is at my locker when I get to school on Monday morning, and even though we're in a crowded hallway, we have the briefest kiss. And even though it happens in a flash, my heart still thuds just as heavily as it did on Saturday, when we didn't have a time limit or an audience. I think about every overdramatic pop song I've ever heard about pounding hearts, and it turns out they aren't actually overdramatic at all.

As I open my locker, a bright blue slip of paper falls out, and when I lean over to pick it up, I see that this is happening to everyone around me too. TALON IS ALMOST HERE, it says, and it has the same eagle icon as last week's flyers.

"This is so weird," I say, crumpling it up.

"Maybe it's something cool," Alex says, and he does his cocked-eyebrow thing again. I want to try for another brief kiss, but already there are so many more people around, and also I'm turning it over in my head how something to do with a boy's eyebrows could make me feel so weak. Another thing from songs that I'm now seeing as total reality. The weakness, that is, not specifically the eyebrows.

"Guys, what is TALON?" Sadie is holding up the slip of paper as she walks over to us. "You know mysteries irritate me."

"Things don't usually stay mysteries for too long," Alex says, and I have the urge to correct him. Lots of mysteries, like Amelia Earhart and Stonehenge and what happened to the pea puree in that episode of *Top Chef,* have never been solved. But I guess TALON is probably not exactly at that level of mystery or importance.

Sadie smirks in my direction. I notice that the tips of her purple hair are now hot pink. "So, what's new, everyone?"

"Your hair looks cool," Alex tells her.

"Thanks! The great Paige Sheraton wasn't happy, of course."

Alex scrunches up his face in confusion. Even this expression makes me want to grab him and kiss him. "Why would Paige Sheraton care about your hair?"

"She's Sadie's mom," I explain. I want to add that, actually, Paige Sheraton doesn't care about Sadie's hair, but if she shows mild surprise at Sadie's new hue, Sadie takes great offense.

We split up in the directions of our classes, and even though I've told Sadie nearly everything on the phone, it's strange to be in person with her and for her to possess all this knowledge.

"Why are you looking at me like that?" she asks as we walk into Ms. Cannon's classroom. "It's my hair, right? I was trying for this whole ombré thing, but I'm worried it didn't come out like I wanted."

"Your hair looks fine," I say, and then I feel bad because Sadie's probably aiming for better than *fine*. "I figured you'd tease me about Alex. Sorry."

"TEASE YOU?"

Everyone already seated stares at Sadie, even though they should be used to her volume by now.

"Jules. We're not in middle school. You're falling in love with a dreamy guy. This is awesome, not tease-worthy, you weirdo."

Her volume's still, well, up, which means everyone seated around us swivels to look. No one asks aloud, but it's as if everyone's asking with their eyes, and this is not what I want. I don't even know how real it's going to be. This is new and crazy and dreamlike, and people wake up from dreams or return to sanity or grow tired of new situations. For Alex and me, it could be any of those things. But also, maybe it won't be.

I expected senior year to be different, because of the *Crest*, and also because, well, senior year is just *supposed* to be different. And of course I'm already filling out practice applications and outlining my college entrance essays.

But now there's Alex.

And my life, like the lunchroom table, seemed like it was already too full for him, but maybe things that I didn't think had any flexibility actually do. And instead of the jittery sensation that normally accompanies my realization that I might have been wrong about something, I still feel like me.

♥ ♥ ♥

We work together again at Stray Rescue on Wednesday. After, we hit Donut Friend; and after that, we walk along York past the clusters of shops and restaurants.

"My mom wants to have you over for dinner," Alex tells me. "She just says we have to unpack more first."

"I don't mind if you aren't unpacked," I say.

"Mom does," he says. "Warning, if it's not obvious: My parents aren't as cool as yours. Dad teaches some advanced mathematics thing I don't even understand, and Mom teaches kindergarten."

"I'm sure they're fine," I say. "And you saw mine at their very coolest."

"I guess I feel like mine are still..." He takes a pause. "Trying to make stuff up to me."

I turn to look at him. "What stuff?"

"The whole Chaos 4 All thing..." He shrugs. "It was a weird life."

"Everyone loved you." I try to say it with a smile he can hear. "The world did."

"Our music," he says. "Our one song, which we didn't even write. Not so many people cared about the next one, and by the third single...Most people don't notice that the world isn't revolving around them, but once it feels like it does, it's hard to go back. And there was other stuff, which I don't even want to talk about."

"I'm sorry," I say.

"I'm fine now," he says. "But then it was hard, I guess. No one tells you how to suddenly *not* be famous."

"No one tells you how to be famous either," I say, and he laughs.

"Nah, people are *hired* to teach you how to be famous. Media training, publicists, all of that. I was good at it. I could teach you how to be famous if I wanted."

"If *you* wanted?"

He turns and kisses me. "If *you* wanted. But I wouldn't do that because it's bullshit and fake, and it's all behind me now. Also, you'd be bad at it."

"What?"

"We'd have to call in the best media-training team in the world," he says. "Your face shows *everything*. You couldn't smile at a dumb entertainment journalist. You made, like, seven different weird faces just in the last thirty seconds."

"Sometimes I feel like my face just does its own thing," I say.

"It's cute," he says. "Don't gain control of your face. I'd miss all your weird looks."

We've made the full loop around and are back at my car. "I should probably go home," I say. "There's so much calculus."

"Sounds scary," he says with a grin. "You should go conquer calculus."

I take Alex home and—after losing plenty of time kissing while parked down the street from his house—head home. Mom's almost finished making dinner, and even Darcy's home before me, and I wait for a lecture on how late I am as they carry the salad, sole, and quinoa to the table. But it's just a normal dinner.

After we eat, I stack my textbooks on the kitchen table and realize I have more homework than usual, and I should have started hours ago. I feel guilty for ignoring it for the extra time I spent with Alex, and then I feel guilty for regretting any moment with him, and then I'm back to feeling like an underachiever, and it just keeps circling.

"Do one thing at a time," Darcy tells me gently after I've shooed them off again and again. "It's not even that late, kiddo. You'll be fine."

"Why aren't you disappointed in me?" I ask while flipping through my economics textbook. "I'm throwing away my academic career for a boy."

"You lost your afternoon because you were spending time with someone you like," she says. "It isn't a crime."

"Brain food," Mom says, bringing me an orange she's already peeled and segmented for me. I don't think oranges are considered brain food by any experts, but the gesture is so nice I just thank her.

"I don't understand why I'm not in trouble," I say. "I'm not responsible."

I don't say the rest of it, which is that I've done plenty of Googling, and my sheer existence must have been really expensive. I once overheard Mom and Darcy say to Paige and Ryan, Sadie's parents, that if it had been financially feasible, *of course* they would have had another baby, but it seemed more important to give me the best life they could. Me! So I have to turn out to be better than average. I don't want to be irresponsible. I want to be worth the money.

"You're the most responsible person I know," Mom says, which makes Darcy furrow her brow. "Sorry, hon, you're fifty-one. You're supposed to be responsible. Relatively speaking, Jules is much higher-ranked."

"If we had a discussion about all the irresponsible things the two of us have done in the name of love," Darcy says, "you'd never finish your homework. So you'll have to trust us that you're in good company."

My face flushes. "Don't say *love.*"

"In the name of *like,* then."

The name of *like* actually seems like a good place to be.

CHAPTER NINE

"You look tired," Sadie says as she sits down next to me in women's history on Friday morning. "Also, hi."

It's not the greatest way to be greeted by your best friend, but she's not wrong. "I was up too late last night," I say.

"Ooh!"

"We were just texting," I say, which is true but also only a tiny glimpse of what that actually means. When it's nighttime and you're in your bedroom and you're manually tapping out messages, even about unromantic topics like Topics in Economics and rescue dogs and cafeteria nachos, you can feel really close to a person.

Before Sadie can ask another question or Ms. Cannon can take roll call, the TV in the classroom turns on automatically. Because the classroom door is open, I can tell that this is happening throughout the school. It's programmed to be possible in case of emergencies or other major news, but no one panics because it's apparently pretty easy to hack. Last year the TVs turned on throughout the school during finals week, and it was just someone's butt. The mystery was never solved, because school administration couldn't just ask students to show their butts to prove it wasn't them.

But this time it isn't a butt. It's a face. Specifically, it's Natalie's face.

"Welcome to TALON," Natalie says, and then the eagle logo and TALON appear on the screen. This doesn't look like the videos Sadie and I used to film at her house with her mom's iPhone. The logo and word look much sharper and better designed on-screen than they did on the flyers. Natalie's wearing a navy pin-striped blazer and a crisp white shirt, and she looks like a real newscaster.

"It's 2016," Natalie continues, as if that fact is news, "and it's time to get all the news that matters to you and your Eagle Vista classmates in a way that fits your life. Go to WeAreTalon .com or the WeAreTalon channel on VidLook to find out more."

"What?" I say aloud, and everyone else is paying such close attention to Natalie that it's like I spoke out of turn in a library. Meg Hartzman even literally shushes me. I look to Sadie for support, but her eyes are on the screen.

I know that back in the eighties someone donated some camera equipment to the school and they tried to make a news program, but according to old issues of the *Crest*, it lasted only a few weeks before imploding. I thought Eagle Vista Academy had learned a lesson from the eighties. Eagle

Vista Academy supposedly honored tradition. *We honor tradition*, it reads on the front page of the official website.

Natalie recaps the first week of school details, like the names of new teachers, the changes made to the school lunch menus, and the upcoming dates of the first events of the year. These are the details we'll be listing in the issue of the *Crest* that comes out next week.

And now, do we even need to? We've been scooped.

"Now I'm going to throw it over to Kevin Fanning for Around-Town, where we'll cover news about not just the school but the larger Eagle Rock community. I'll let Kevin tell you more."

The video seamlessly cuts to Kevin, who was also conspicuously absent from the *Crest* meeting this week. I flip to a blank page in my notebook and jot down the names of all of last year's staff members who are missing from this year's crew. Jesse Walters shows up after Kevin, and then Joramae Reyes. I check them off my list as they appear. They're all wearing professional attire that looks good on camera—even Jesse, whose normal uniform is a ragged band T-shirt and beyond-faded jeans.

The camera finally cuts back to Natalie, and I exhale a teensy bit of relief that not every single person on my list has appeared.

"Last on our program, a new segment from a new student."

It's another perfectly edited cut, and then another face is on the screen.

Alex.

"What?" I say, again, aloud, and louder. This time, Sadie turns to me with her eyes wide. Her expression matches my emotions.

"Shhhh!" Meg says, again.

"Hi, I'm Alex Powell, and this is"—a logo appears on-screen as he says it—"Alex 4 All."

I realize he's wearing the same shirt as he was the day we met. His first day in school, the second day of the school year. I wonder if TALON meets when the *Crest* does, because that would have been the same day as well. I think of Alex's sugar-coated lips as he confided all about his past to me. And I realize that by then he'd already filmed this. He'd told Natalie and company way before he'd told me. At least a full twenty-four hours. Alex knew all about this airing today when I was curled up in my bed sending him messages last night.

As Alex throws it back to Natalie, Sadie whispers, Sadie-style, "Are you okay?"

"I'm fine," I say just a little too loudly. It's for everyone else's benefit, but it must have sounded believable because Sadie turns away from me, and then I'm just stuck with my own thoughts in my own brain as Natalie says that she'll see us in a week. The credits roll, and every person I hadn't yet checked off the list is there in some behind-the-scenes capacity.

Those people all chose to work with Natalie at the helm, not me.

"Now that *that's* over, let's try to get some work accomplished today, shall we?" Ms. Cannon's tone is just annoyed enough for me to briefly feel love toward her. But then she takes roll and moves onto women in ancient Egypt and she sounds just as annoyed, so the love in my heart is gone as quickly as it arrived.

The sound of everyone's pens flying across papers jolts me out of whatever state I didn't know I was in. I know everyone else hasn't had their entire world splintered into...world shards, but I wish I could yell at them for just going on with their lives. With *Egypt*.

I raise my hand, even though it seems like Ms. Cannon is in the middle of something at least fairly important. I'm dealing with something that's unfairly important.

"Miss McAllister-Morgan, if this isn't an emergency, I suggest you hold all your questions until I'm through this section."

"This is an emergency," I say, even though anytime a girl throws around the word *emergency*, people will assume it's something to do with your period. "May I please be excused?"

Ms. Cannon sighs loudly but dismisses me. I grab all my things and run out the door, down the hall, and up the stairs to Mr. Wheeler's room. He's in the midst of what looks like freshman English—everyone's super young and staring at him like all his words are important.

"Hi, Jules," he says. "This is a surprise. Is everything all right?"

"*No.* Obviously everything isn't all right," I say, and his eyes go huge and round behind his glasses. "TALON?"

"Oh, that." He chuckles. "Pretty cool, huh?"

"NO," I say, again.

"Jules." He sighs and gestures to the hallway. We walk out of the classroom, and he shuts the door behind him. I want to say he probably shouldn't trust a whole class of freshmen in an enclosed room, but that is far from my priority right now.

"They scooped us!" I say. "Every single thing we'd cover in the paper next week, they've already done it."

"Not everything," he says. "We can go much more in depth in an issue of the *Crest* than they can in ten minutes once a week."

"No one will read us now," I say. "They're destroying a hundred-and-four-year-old tradition."

"Do you have a class right now?" he asks.

"Of course I have a class right now. This is much more important."

"Jules, get back to your class. We can talk later."

"Mr. Wheeler—"

"I'll see you in fourth period, Jules," he says, and walks back into the classroom, shutting the door behind him. I stare at the closed door with my mouth open for probably much longer than is even borderline acceptable, and turn around to head back to women's history. But if I couldn't sit still in there before talking to Mr. Wheeler, how can I manage now? I thought of all people, someone with old-man sweaters and an antique wristwatch would care about legacy and tradition. I was never exactly thrilled that it felt like Mr. Wheeler and I might have a lot of things in common, but it's actually worse to realize that, except our semi-shared backyard, we don't.

I've never skipped a class before. But I walk to the library and find out that no one even challenges me as I slip in and take a seat at one of the private-study desks. Could I have been a truant this whole time? I guess real truants don't hang out at the school library. Probably also they don't refer to themselves as truants.

Maybe I was just so excited about all the good stuff with Alex that I missed this. I get out my phone and scroll through all my texts. For someone I've only known for less than two weeks, there are a lot to go back through. But Alex didn't mention TALON, Natalie, or extracurriculars at all.

I wonder if I'm naïve to think once someone's tongue has been inside your mouth, they owe you at least that much information? Yes, all right, fine, that much I know is naïve. On TV, people sleep with each other just to get secrets or betray someone else or, even, just because they want to. Kissing is nothing.

Sadie's at my locker when I arrive after first period. "Are you okay? For real?"

"For real, no."

She gives me a hug and kisses my cheek. In the flash of that moment she's just like her mom, but since I don't want to turn a sweet moment into what Sadie might interpret as a mean one, I keep that to myself.

"He *lied to me*, Sadie."

"Okay, he didn't tell you about their stupid show, big deal." But even as she says it, I can tell from her eyes that she knows as well as I do that it *is* a big deal. "Aaaand here he comes right now."

"Noooo." I jam my women's history books into my locker and attempt to extract my Latin textbook. "Why can't I do this faster?"

"Hey," Alex says. "What did you think?"

"She's in a hurry," Sadie says in a chilly voice. "Come on, Jules."

I yank the book as hard as I can, and whatever it was caught on gives way and the book shoots across the hallway.

"Ow!" someone yells, and I see that it was Justin making his way over to Sadie.

"I'm so sorry," I tell him as he brings my book back to me.

"I didn't know Latin was so dangerous," Alex says.

Sadie shoots him a warning look before tending to Justin's injury. I tuck the book under my arm and take off down the hallway.

"Jules, wait up." Alex strides up next to me. "What's going on?"

"What do you *think*?"

"Uh, I seriously have no idea."

I reach the doorway of Latin and decide to walk right in. I'm not expecting Alex to follow me. Everyone already seated stares at him like a celebrity. Okay, technically, I guess he kind of *is* a celebrity.

"Can you just talk to me?" he asks. "I'm really confused."

"I'm in class," I say. "And I don't want to talk to you."

He sighs but doesn't move for a few moments. "Fine."

And then he's gone.

♥ ♥ ♥

In fourth period, I assume that even with Mr. Wheeler's complete lack of understanding of the gravity of the TALON situation, the rest of the staff will be in my corner.

And it's true that everyone is talking about TALON.

"Natalie looked really pretty," one sophomore says.

"I think it's so cool Alex Powell can make fun of himself!" says a junior.

"The graphics looked crazy professional," Thatcher says, and then, when I glare at him, "What?"

"I know that TALON looked very impressive, but we need what we're doing to still matter," I say. If I were in a TV show, the music would swell and I'd rise to my feet and deliver a moving monologue about tradition and journalism and our founding staff back in 1912. People would feel so much they'd *cry*.

I know better than to try it, though.

"Hey, guys, what we're doing still matters," Mr. Wheeler says. "Maybe print media is dying out, maybe it isn't. Let's just keep doing a good job. The *Crest* is funded through at least this year, so if we're going out, we'll go out with a bang."

"*If*?" I realize I'm yelling, again, so I take a deep breath.

"Don't you care that something that's mattered for so long could *just disappear*? We're an endangered species. Think of how much people do to protect the South China tiger."

"I have literally never heard of the South China tiger," Mr. Wheeler says. "But I know you and your family are big animal lovers, Jules. Let's get moving on the next issue. Has everyone turned in their pieces?"

The room springs into action, which is a moment that, no matter how many hundreds of times I experience it, feels beautiful and perfect. The motion and buzz give me energy, and I'm sure I can figure out a way to have this for the rest of my life. The *Crest* is really only my beginning and I know it.

But that doesn't mean I want the *Crest* to go away once I've graduated and literally moved on. And I can't believe that it feels like no one else would even notice.

♥ ♥ ♥

At lunch I head straight to our table because I have no appetite. Justin is sitting with his jeans pushed up to his knee, showing off the bruise from the book attack this morning. I guess in case I wanted to feel worse about myself, now I can.

"I'm really sorry," I say. Sadie's been dating Justin since late into last school year, but even though we sit near each other and occasionally go to the same things with Sadie, I don't really know him. We're definitely not *friends*.

"It's all good," he says. "It's badass, right?"

"I guess," I say, though badassery isn't one of my expert topics.

"It's super badass." Sadie sits down with two trays and slides one over to Justin. If he couldn't stand in line because of his injury, I'll feel, somehow, even more horrible, so I'll just assume she's being a really, really nice girlfriend today.

"I was struck down by the Latin language," Justin says. "What's Latin for *legs*?"

"*Crura*," Em and I chorus.

Sadie gives me a very direct look. "Are you doing okay?"

I start to say I'm fine, and then I start to say that I'm not, but I have no idea what I actually am. So I just shrug.

"I don't think it's a big deal," Thatcher says as he takes his lunch out of a perfectly folded brown paper bag. "They did that thing back in the eighties. It failed. Maybe this one will too. Or it won't. It's fine."

"Don't be so Zen," I say, and I guess it comes out rudely because everyone stares wide-eyed at me. Even Thatcher the Zen Master. "I'm sorry."

Great. Now I've injured one friend's boyfriend's leg and another's boyfriend's feelings. I am a danger to all boyfriends.

"Taco Day!" Alex appears with his lunch tray piled high with tacos and sides. I don't like to stereotype by gender, but boys eat so much. "You guys didn't even spoil the surprise."

"Every other Friday," Justin says with a nod, and then he and Alex do a fist bump. Over tacos? When *things* are going on?

Boys make no sense.

"Why are you here?" I ask.

"Yeah, Alex," Sadie says. "Why are you here?"

"I, uhhh, I sit here?" He slides right into a chair and starts plowing into a taco. Maybe he doesn't know this is serious business or maybe he's a jerk. Right now it's hard to tell.

CHAPTER TEN

I drive to Sadie's after my short top-level-staff-only meeting for the *Crest* after school. It's meant to be when we lock down final articles and layout, but if the meetings have run smoothly all week during fourth period, there's rarely a lot left to accomplish after school on Fridays.

It should have felt like sending the paper off to the printer so quickly was a victory. But thanks to TALON, it just feels like one more sign what we're doing doesn't even matter.

Sadie and I already had plans, which were to consist roughly of ordering huge amounts of food, probably rewatching all the Chaos 4 All videos, and definitely talking about all the things that just a week ago I never expected to experience my senior year of high school.

But while we're browsing online menus we're definitely not talking about attractive eyebrows or parked-car kissing or how your brain just knows how to churn out love-type feelings when you were pretty sure you wouldn't have to worry about it for years.

"He can't think things are actually fine, right?" I ask. "He was acting like he wanted me to think he thought that. But he couldn't *actually* think that. Could he?"

"Boys can think a lot of things," Sadie says. "But Alex seems very sincere. I seriously think he has no clue. So I'm leaning toward Thai, but I could do sushi."

"You know I hate the idea of delivery sushi," I say. "Thai is fine, as long as we can compromise on spice level."

"Mild," she says immediately.

"For the millionth time, mild is *not* a compromise! It starts out mild."

"No," Sadie says, gesturing to her iPad screen, "it starts out with NO SPICES AT ALL. And you know it's not my fault! It's genetics."

I've never actually told Sadie that I hate talking about genetics, so I don't hold it against her. I even let her select *mild* for the seasoning in half the dishes we order. My own genetics feel like such a wild card, though. I'm more of a project than a person, really. Darcy's egg, Mom's uterus, and some stranger's...stuff. I can barely think about Mom's uterus, so hopefully it's all right to think of the rest as just *stuff.* Mom and Darcy swear that his profile was basically the man version of Mom (Italian and Irish ancestry, shorter than average, above-average intelligence, lover of dogs and the *New Yorker*—I still don't believe that his profile actually was specific enough to

98

list the *New Yorker*, but I know it's all part of the fairy tale they tell of my beginning, so I let it slide). I don't want to meet the provider of the stuff, but I do wonder about him sometimes. It seems to me like normal well-adjusted guys have better things to do with their stuff.

"Can you tell Justin not to be friends with Alex?" I ask, though the second it's out of my mouth I can hear how crazy that sounds.

"No," she says. "What if Justin told me not to be friends with someone? You'd kick his ass. Or at least throw another book at his legs."

"Are you guys going to be in here all night?" Sadie's little brother, Jon, walks into the room carrying a tall stack of Blu-rays. He's only fourteen, but he's been obsessed with kung fu and other martial arts movies for years now.

"Yes," Sadie says. "Watch those in your room."

"My screen is too small!" he says.

"That sounds like a personal problem," she says.

I'm so glad I'm an only child.

By the time our food shows up, we've struck an agreement with Jon that he can have the family room until ten. Sadie and I arrange the food on the kitchen table. When we were younger, we read an article online about how to properly order a Thai meal. So even though it's just the two of us, we have tom kha soup, chicken satay, a seafood salad, two different curries, pad see ew, a mountain of sticky rice, and another mountain of mango and coconut milk with more sticky rice.

"Remember how much food we ordered when I broke up with Milo last year?" Sadie asks. "And we weren't even trying to respect a cuisine's traditions."

"I'm not sure I can say I broke up with Alex. It's not like we were in an official relationship," I say.

"It counts," she says.

"I thought he liked me," I say.

"I think he did like you," Sadie says. "I mean, DOES like you. He's just being stupid about TALON, as if it wouldn't mean anything to you."

"It's not just that," I say. "It's that he acted like we had a secret when it wasn't a secret. He told me about being in Chaos 4 All like it was just between us. Obviously I knew people knew, but like gossip. Not from him. Now it's the whole reference for his stupid video column? And if he actually thought TALON wasn't a big deal, why did he hide it from me?"

"I'm sorry, Jules," she says.

"And he says he's done, you know, being famous and being in the spotlight. If that was true, why would he..." I hope Sadie thinks I'm crying from the green curry sauce and not my feelings. "What if he was just telling me what he thought I wanted to hear? What if I don't even *know him*?"

"I'm sorry," she says again, and she holds my hand, but she doesn't tell me I'm wrong.

"This feels *awful*," I say. "I was right to put off boys. They're more stress than I need."

"Boys aren't some monolithic stress machine," she says.

"Justin causes me very little stress. He sends me cute messages, he brings me snacks sometimes, and he's really good at kissing and everything else. I'm seriously sorry this whole Alex thing went down the way it did, but you can't blame boys."

I know Sadie's right, but I decide to mull it over instead of just agreeing with her.

♥ ♥ ♥

The next morning, I stop off at Swork for coffee before driving to Stray Rescue. After saying hi to Tricia, I make my way down the row of kennels. But as I'm about to wave to Santiago, the person next to him turns around.

"What are you doing here?" My voice comes out all pinched and squeaky, and the dogs bark a chorus of excitement or maybe it's annoyance.

Alex shrugs, and a grin spreads across his face like it's time-released. "The same as you? Walking dogs?"

"But we're—we're not—you're—TALON—"

"I *like* doing this, Jules," he says, and I hate how my name sounds in his voice. It rings with an intimacy we're never, ever going to have now. "And Santiago said how they're never too overrun with volunteers, and I didn't have plans today, so..."

"Fine," I say. "Be a good person to dogs. I don't care. Dogs have no real dreams to destroy."

He kind of laughs and shakes his head. "Jules..."

"Here you go, Alex," Santiago says, bringing a Doberman

mix over. "He's big but gentle, so I know you'll be able to handle him on your own."

I quickly leash up the nearest dog and glance at her name (Hildy) before rushing outside. Unfortunately Alex is right with me.

"Look," he says, "I wasn't trying to...destroy your dreams. I'm not even sure how I am."

"I literally don't understand how you could think anything that happened is okay," I say, trying to hold back Hildy, who's pulling at her leash to sniff Alex's Doberman.

"Could we just talk?" he asks. "Please?"

"I don't know what we could talk about. You made me feel like the stupidest girl on the planet, and you're part of something that's going to ruin the only thing I looked forward to for my senior year." I can hear how hyperbolic my statements are turning, but Alex should know how his actions affect others. Affect *me*.

"I thought you'd like it," he says. "You like extracurriculars."

"Not ones that are out to destroy me."

"Fine," he says. "I'll leave you alone."

"Good!"

"Great!"

We walk the same path, though, around the same blocks. When Alex's dog stops to poop, so does Hildy. Alex and I have to use the same trash can to throw away the poop bags. Santiago keeps leashing dogs for Alex as quickly as I can leash my own. We're locked in this constant pattern, leashing and walking and throwing away poop. Just a few days ago it all would have seemed incredibly romantic.

Now it's a battle.

♥ ♥ ♥

The *Crest* comes out on Mondays. Once we're through this week and the chosen freshman have officially joined staff, they'll be the ones to spend their Monday lunches handing out papers, so the sophomores are handling for now. It's fair because during fourth period we get to order giant pizzas from Big Mama's & Papa's, so no one's going hungry, and the whole staff is camping out in Mr. Wheeler's room. This is basically the only time all week when we don't have to panic about next week's issue. We'll enjoy these fleeting moments.

(I actually enjoy the stressful moments too, but I'm trying to be relatable to the rest of the staff, who don't seem to crave deadlines and panic the way I do.)

Thatcher is showing me his portfolio-in-progress for his art school applications when the sophomores start filing in with leftover papers. Normally, the copies get stacked on the corner of Mr. Wheeler's desk. We've had it down to a science for years; print the right number of copies, and there's no fear of having too many wasted afterward.

But I immediately notice that the stacks look too tall for

Mr. Wheeler's desk. I abandon Thatcher as well as my garlic-and-basil pizza to direct them to the table where the papers had been dropped off this morning.

The leftover newspapers cover the table. In fact, if you didn't look carefully, it would be easy to believe that we were exactly where we started this morning.

"Jules was right," Carlos says, surveying the piles. "It seems like no one cares."

"No one cares!" Kari Ellison, a sophomore, says. "People were like, 'I don't care!'"

The whole staff begins drifting to the back of the room to survey this tangible proof of Eagle Vista Academy's disinterest.

"See?" I say. "A tradition is dying."

"We'll print fewer copies next week," Mr. Wheeler says between chomps of pizza. There's grease, somehow, on his forehead. Come on, Mr. Wheeler. If you can't inspire us, can't you at least eat pizza correctly? "It won't look so depressing then, guys."

"But it won't change the fact that it *is* depressing," I say. "Is TALON really that great?"

Everyone murmurs embarrassed-sounding affirmatives.

"Okay, fine," I contend, "but does it have to *replace* us? Can't we *do something*?"

"Yeah," says Marisa Johnston, a junior I'm fairly certain already has her eye on the editor position for next year. "Can't we fight back?"

"I guess I didn't care about tradition," Thatcher says. "Sorry, Jules. But I do care about not letting TALON win. This means—"

"Can I say it?" I interrupt. I have *always* wanted a moment like this, and it's here! Maybe TALON has actually given me a gift. I get to be the underdog, and everyone knows that the underdog is the one to root for. I've been gearing up my whole life to be the underdog.

Thatcher grins at me. "Go for it. You've earned it."

"This means war."

CHAPTER ELEVEN

We'd rather get Kevin or Joramae back, but we go for Amanda Lynde first. On-camera talent probably couldn't give up the allure of the audience. Not yet, at least. Amanda is just listed as *Crew*. It doesn't sound alluring to any of us.

"How's TALON?" I ask, walking up to her while she's at her locker.

"Oh, it's okay," she says, glancing back at me. "Congrats on getting editor; that's cool."

Carlos appears on her right side. "It'll look really good to colleges that you're doing stuff on VidLook," he says, somehow infusing each subsequent word with more and more sarcasm.

"Well, it's a whole show," Amanda says. "It's not just Vid-Look. Plus we'll be building up a large following. I'll explain it on my applications."

Thatcher walks up on her left side. He doesn't do it with quite the ninja panache Carlos managed, but it's still effective. "We still need an extracurriculars editor," he says. "That sounds better than crew, you have to admit."

"We can give you more to do on the paper," I say. "With a better title."

"Natalie'll be mad," she says.

I can't help it. "Who cares about Natalie!"

Thatcher and Carlos glare at me.

"What Jules means," Thatcher says, "is that this is about you, not Natalie, and not us. Since you'll have a better title and more to do, you can look better to Stanford."

Amanda closes her eyes for just a moment at the mention of Stanford.

"Who knows what'll happen if you stay with TALON," Carlos says.

"Are you guys gonna beat me up?" Amanda asks in a soft voice.

"No!" the three of us shout simultaneously.

"We want what's best for you," I say. I sound like Darcy, if Darcy wasn't a sincere person.

"I'll think about it," she says.

We start to disperse.

"Wait!" Amanda says. "My little sister says she was rejected."

"We don't 'reject' people," I say. "It's just that we can't choose every single freshman who submits."

"It would be a nice bonding experience for us," she says.

"Before you go away to Stanford," Thatcher says.

"Yes, exactly."

I go through the freshman submissions in my head, though I can't specifically remember another Lynde. It's dangerous just agreeing to this, because while it's true that we didn't technically *reject* everyone, there were some pretty bad pieces in there. What if the other Lynde sister wrote the "investigative" "report" on the most popular parking spaces, or the op-ed about buying a real live eagle to keep on school grounds? And I'm not even sure if we can let in a freshman after the fact. She'd still have to change her schedule around, and that would require Mr. Wheeler's sign-off. We're probably already pushing it with Amanda.

"She's in," Carlos says. "We'll take care of everything."

I hold out my hand because it feels like we're all supposed to shake, but no one else does, so I pretend I was just about to push my hair behind my ears in an unnecessarily complicated fashion.

♥ ♥ ♥

As a new student at Eagle Vista Academy, I'm looking forward to sharing in school spirit. And what could bring the student body together as well as something big, bold, and exciting?

Tessa Lynde didn't just submit an essay about a real live eagle; she did so in a dull way. And therefore, that night it takes me longer to write up a pitch on why we must add Tessa to our team than it does to do any of my individual homework assignments. When I spot Mr. Wheeler outside, I take the dogs into the backyard and pretend to casually notice him. Obviously, I could have talked to him today at our weekly after-school meeting, but I don't want this to seem calculated.

"Hi, Mr. Wheeler," I say in the tone I normally reserve for liaison duty. "Are you having a good night?"

"Hi, Jules, and I guess it's all right." He eyes Peanut, who's circling Daisy in rapid circles. "That guy's wound up, huh."

"Always. So I thought, if you had a moment, we could discuss a couple of *Crest*-related items."

"Jules..." Mr. Wheeler shrugs. "I'm not sure if we should mix school business and personal time."

Mr. Wheeler has sat at my kitchen table on *multiple occasions* discussing *his love life*. With my *parents*.

He's not getting out of this so easily.

"As you know, TALON took a huge bite out of our readership yesterday," I say as if he'd agreed to this talk. "We're looking for inventive ways to make up for that loss."

"Jules, I was in the room when you declared war," he says.

"We talked to Amanda Lynde, and she'd love to come back," I say. "Since we haven't officially filled the extracurriculars editor position yet—"

"I thought we discussed Jordan—"

"And because Amanda's absence is so profoundly felt"—I place a hand over my heart—"we think it's a great idea."

"Sure," Mr. Wheeler says with far less investment than I'd like from him. "Have her see me before first period tomorrow morning and I'll get her the paperwork to switch into our class period."

"Wonderful. And talking to Amanda jogged my memory, since one of the freshmen I very nearly recommended for the staff has the same last name. And for the sake of sisterly solidarity, I thought—especially with our numbers down this year—we could reconsider Tessa Lynde as well."

"What piece did Tessa submit?" he asks.

"The incredibly inventive piece about increasing school spirit," I say, because I am not speaking the words *real, live,* or *eagle.*

Mr. Wheeler sighs, and his shoulders seem to lurch downward in the faded Death Cab for Cutie T-shirt he's wearing. He turns to head back inside his little guest cottage. "Fine, Jules. Have her see me tomorrow morning too."

"Yes," I say to myself. "Victory will be *mine.*"

"Jules," Mr. Wheeler says. "I can hear you."

CHAPTER TWELVE

Sadie's at my locker the next morning. It's normal, but I feel like I've barely seen her this week so far. The *Crest* has monopolized my free time, which I'd expected this year anyway, though of course not in this way.

"I hate to tell you this," she says seriously, and I nearly drop my books instead of transferring them successfully from my backpack to my locker. Sadie sounds overdramatic all the time, sure, but serious?

"What's going on?"

"Oh my god, your face." She laughs and offers me a piece of the scone she's eating. I suppose people don't eat scones during emergencies. "I was just going to say that I think the boys are all, like, officially best friends or bros or whatever now."

"*Bros?*" I ask.

"I know you wish he'd disappear from the school or at least our lunch table, but..." Sadie shoves more of the scone at me. "I'm sorry."

"I'm fine," I say after another bite of scone. "I'll destroy him."

"Uh, whoa," Em says, walking up to us. "Everything okay over here?"

I'm about to say yes, but Alex walks by. When someone breaks your heart, something about that person physically should be required to change. He shouldn't get to keep his wavy brown hair or his soulful brown eyes and most definitely not his eyebrows that have their very own seduction powers. He shouldn't look like a boy I thought I could fall in love with.

"Jules," Sadie says, "eyes on the prize."

"*What?*"

"His destruction," she says. "Right?"

I couldn't ask for a better friend than Sadie, and I know it.

"Right," I say. "But..."

"Let's get to class," Sadie says.

Em doesn't look suspicious that Sadie suddenly cares about promptness, but I eye her as she pulls me down the hallway.

"But what?" she asks, because Sadie can pick up conversations from days ago like no time has passed.

"But I hate seeing him, and I hate feeling like this, and I wish he wasn't bros or whatever with half the lunch table. That's all."

"That's more than enough," she says. "You're allowed to still feel crappy about this, you know. When Isaac dumped me, I felt crappy for forever. Wait, is that not helpful?"

"You're always helpful," I say. I know I'm lucky to have

Sadie in my life. When the two of us talk, it feels like I require half the words I normally do. Maybe it's just because we grew up together that I never have to worry about her understanding me, but whatever the reason, I'm glad that this is how it is.

Also, of course, Sadie understands boys. And I figured that would come in handy someday in the future, but now that the future is here, it's even more of a relief than I would have guessed.

"We can do something after school," she says as we walk into women's history. "If you want to hang out and talk." If Sadie minds that she's usually the one pushing plans on me and rarely the other way around, it never shows. She's the one who's figured out how to combine achieving goals and also having fun, and we both know it.

"I have Stray Rescue," I say. "And, not that I would have skipped it before, but I really can't now, with Alex volunteering on my schedule."

"And Stray Rescue is *your* turf!"

"Exactly," I say. "I can't be about talk; I have to be about *action*."

"Okay, so what about after Stray Rescue?" Sadie asks. "Come over! Mom's cooking...well, Mom's cooking something. You know how she gets when she's between jobs. You have no idea how many scones are at our house right now."

I'd rather go home and make more lists about how to destroy TALON, but it feels right to say yes to Sadie. Also I should probably complete the tasks on one of the lists before

I compose any more of them, and I can't move too quickly or I'll make Mr. Wheeler suspicious. More suspicious? I have never thought of him as particularly savvy, but this is all uncharted territory.

When I get to Stray Rescue that afternoon, I'm prepared to see Alex. I just *have* to be. There's no other option but quitting—and I would never quit. And, also, I'm getting used to it. Besides our classes together, which until recently felt like a wish granted by fate, we share a way-too-crowded lunch table. I don't know why Alex has stuck around, considering that we're over. Oh my god, is it some kind of "bros before hos" thing? Real live boys don't actually say things like that...right?

"Hi, Jules," Tricia greets me as I walk inside Stray Rescue. "Your boyfriend brought quite a crowd today, huh?"

"He's not my boyfriend," I say, and I wish I could reach into the air and pull back my words, or at the least my snappy tone. "Sorry, it's just that...he's not."

Tricia's expression softens. "I'm sorry, Jules."

I'm more embarrassed that Tricia can see my heartbreak than curious about her mention of Alex's crowd of people. But once I make my way back, there they are. There's a sophomore I've seen around but don't know, Arvin Mercado is manning a video camera, and Natalie's standing nearby making notes on a clipboard.

"Hello, Julia," Natalie says without any emotion. This normally wouldn't send up any red flags, but this whole scene is a red flag.

"Hello, TALON," I say.

"Hey, Jules." Santiago pops up behind all the people and equipment. "Pretty cool that we're going to be on your school's TV show."

"Let me just get a dog and go," I say.

"FYI," Natalie says, pronouncing each letter in a perfectly clipped newscaster manner, "I'm not stupid, Julia. I know Amanda's sudden defection to the *Crest* was your doing."

"Defection?" I roll my eyes. "Amanda has been a member of the *Crest* for three years. She's a member of the *Crest* still. She's not the one I'd call a defector."

The sophomore I don't know tentatively points the camera toward me. "Should we get her on film?"

"Definitely not," Natalie says. "Julia isn't a part of this story."

I stare at Alex, who's standing silently next to Santiago, almost as if someone hit a pause button on him. He must be used to waiting for a record button to be pressed before activating human behavior.

"I wouldn't know about this place if not for Jules," Alex says, back in motion. "She should get to be on camera."

"I don't *want* to be on camera," I say. "I don't do this to get attention; I do this to help dogs and our community."

"Good," Natalie says. "Not 'good' about dogs and community, which I don't care about, but we'd have to adjust the lighting if you were on camera. You would look"—she gestures to my hair and face—"washed out."

"I use a strong sunblock," I say. "It's never too early to take care of your skin."

"Then I guess you're built for print," she says.

I wish I felt like more of a formidable opponent against Natalie today, but she had the element of surprise on her side, as well as a TALON-appropriate wardrobe. Since it's a Stray Rescue day, I'm casual in jeans and a striped T-shirt, but of course Natalie is in a perfectly crisp blazer over a bright white button-down shirt. I wonder what Alex thinks of her; she did bring him aboard TALON his very first day of school. Natalie must have persuasive skills, on top of a newscaster wardrobe. I worry he can't resist that, and then I worry that I'm worried.

But, of course, I'm not here to battle Natalie and the rest of TALON today. So I leash up the closest dog I see—a pit mix named Leonard—and head outside. Footsteps thud up behind me, and Leonard and I spin around to see Alex dashing toward me.

"Jules," he says, and stops to catch his breath. *Don't find it adorable, don't find it adorable.* "I want to help dogs and the community too. I thought if I did a piece, people might want to adopt dogs, or at least volunteer here too."

"Fine," I say.

"Look," he says, "I don't want attention."

"You told me all about people who'd only do something like this when the camera's on them," I say. "This feels exactly like that."

"Jules, don't think that," he says. "Even if we aren't—"

"I can think whatever I want." I turn from him and continue walking with Leonard. There's probably a huge chance I'll end up in the background of the TALON piece, so I keep distracting myself with positive thoughts—*Doughnuts! Hanging out with Sadie! A sale at J.Crew this weekend!*—so that when I'm in the background, my face won't give away any of my other feelings.

When you hear about war heroes, they don't emerge victorious from easily won battles. TALON might have all the attention now, but I won't let my side down. I will hold my face at neutral while cameras are around. And before long, I will win this war.

I don't want to think about what will happen if I don't.

CHAPTER THIRTEEN

On Friday I'm ready when the TV screen lowers and Natalie's face appears. TALON might be making their best effort to end almost everything important at Eagle Vista Academy, but they're not going to keep surprising me.

This week it doesn't feel like they've scooped us, because their stories have nothing to do with what we're working on for next week's issue. They have an interview with a new science teacher, but we already listed his credentials and welcome message in this week's issue. Kevin tours the school, which looks fine on camera, but we all walk through it every day, so it's definitely not a scoop. It's barely even a story, Kevin. Over at the *Crest*, we're actually exploring the historical architecture *in depth*.

Alex's segment is last, again. I've silently informed every cell in my body that I'll have to see his face in a place I love on a screen in front of all my women's history classmates.

I'm still afraid I may have audibly taken a giant breath when the camera pans out and Santiago talks about the history of Highland Park Stray Rescue.

"Awww!" nearly the entire class choruses as the camera pans to dog after dog. Leonard's on-screen, and so is Lola, and to be honest I may have been one of the *awww*ers. I think most people are scientifically programmed to loudly react this way to the unexpected appearance of dogs.

"Are you surviving?" Sadie faux-whispers, reaching over to my desk and squeezing my hand. "I'm trying to survive twice as hard so you don't have to."

"That makes no sense," I say, but I don't let go either.

In our top-level staff meeting after school, we sign off on Monday's issue pretty quickly. I can tell from how Mr. Wheeler's shoving stuff into his messenger bag that he thinks the meeting is about to disperse.

"I think it's time to launch our next plan of attack at TALON," I say, flipping through my red notebook. "If they—"

" 'Plan of attack'?" Mr. Wheeler stops treating his bag like a garbage receptacle and stares at us. "Hey, guys, I know you all care about the paper. I care about the paper too. But—wait, what was the first plan of attack?"

I know Carlos will be the first to break under any pressure—I can just feel it—so I lock eyes with him. Thatcher's doing the same thing.

"Guys, let's head out. The paper will be fine this year. Next year you'll all be away at college, and you won't care about it anymore, trust me."

"I'm actually planning on staying local," Carlos says. "UCLA has a really good program in—"

"Guys, get out of here."

The three of us head into the hallway, where Mr. Wheeler rushes by us a moment later. I've never seen him in such a hurry; there should be cartoon motion lines blinking from behind him.

"Maybe he has a date," Carlos says.

"Ew," I say. "I hope not."

"Mr. Wheeler lives in her backyard," Thatcher tells Carlos.

"Not my backyard, my neighbor's backyard," I say. "And in a guesthouse; he's not out in a tent. But it's bad enough. Once I thought he was out of town and I went outside in my pajamas, but he'd gotten home early. Your teacher should never see you in your pajamas."

"They weren't, like, sexy pajamas, were they?" Carlos asks with fear in his eyes.

"Dude, you can't ask her that," Thatcher says.

"I'm gay, I can ask!" he says. "Eh, I guess it's still a creepy question?"

"It's still a creepy question," I say. "But to clarify, *no*. They were not. They're regular pajamas with little bumblebees printed on them."

Thatcher raises an eyebrow. "Bumblebees?"

"They're whimsical!" I walk down the hallway to my locker. The guys continue to trail me. "I hate that Mr. Wheeler isn't taking any of this seriously."

"He's right that next year I probably won't care about this," Thatcher says. "But I do care *now* about crushing those pretentious idiots."

Thatcher says this while wearing bright orange glasses, a Xeno & Oaklander T-shirt, skinny jeans rolled up just above his ankles, and oxfords without socks.

I assume we'll separate, like we did last week after our meeting ended, but instead we walk down the street to Swork. Since I assume we might get loud with our righteous anger, we take a seat with our drinks at an outside table.

"Wheeler's a problem," Carlos says. "If we really want to bring TALON down, we need him out of the picture."

"Oh my god," I say. "Are you going to have him killed?"

Carlos and Thatcher laugh at me for what feels like twenty minutes while I figure out that of course that wasn't what Carlos meant.

"We need meetings somewhere off-campus," Carlos says.

"Non-Wheeler meetings," Thatcher says, sounding very ready to engage in this battle for someone with more of a Zen reputation. I like this side of Thatcher. Or at least I relate to it more. "That means your house is out, Jules."

"My house is fine," Carlos says. "Email everyone this weekend. It'll be best coming from you, as our leader."

♥ ♥ ♥

to: the-crest-staff@emailgroups.com
from: julia.b.mcallister-morgan@email.com
subject: Operation TALON

Hello team,

Obviously, our entire staff would like to ensure that the *Crest* not only remains relevant but thrives, with its future at Eagle Vista Academy assured.

Mr. Wheeler, while a qualified and involved faculty advisor, doesn't approve of the rivalry with TALON and therefore is now not necessarily invested in best practices for keeping the *Crest* going beyond our time at E.V.A.

If your availability allows it, on Tuesdays after our standard staff meeting, we will reconvene at Carlos Esquivel's house* for plan-ning and strategy to eliminate TALON from E.V.A.**

Please reply and let me know if you'll be able to attend second-ary meetings.***

Yours,
JBM-M

*See Google Maps link.
**Snacks will be provided.
***After some research I've determined that there's no way to make an email self-destruct. So after replying, please delete this email.

♥ ♥ ♥

On Monday, the freshmen should be handing out new issues of the *Crest* at lunch, but this isn't time to mess around. It's no longer acceptable to entrust the distribution of our century-old paper to *fourteen-year-olds.*

I haven't handed out the paper in three years, but I've handed out flyers at Stray Rescue's annual dog fair, and I've learned some lessons in optimizing this process. Friendly eye contact is key. It's important to be confident, but not pushy. And it's important to make whatever you're handing out appear to be a benefit, not something you're trying to dispose of.

I'm not worried about my confidence level, especially since I did well at this weekend's J.Crew sale and am wearing a new striped shirt over new gray pants. Darcy even let me borrow one of her nicest pairs of flats. Em stops me on my way to Mr. Wheeler's classroom to get the papers and hands me a bottle in a paper bag.

"Is this *alcohol?*" I whisper, and Em laughs.

"Of course not. It's caffeine. Give out those papers, girl."

I chug the Mexican Coke on my way and grab the biggest stack off the table in Mr. Wheeler's room. The pure cane sugar soda courses through my system, and I feel taller and brighter than usual.

"Would you like a copy of the *Crest?*" I ask students as I make my way down the corridor. My eyes are crinkled with my smile, and I offer plenty of reasons people should take the paper. "It has next week's lunch menu!" "It has next month's athletic schedule!" "You can learn a lot about the history of the brickwork in the courtyard!"

A couple of people take copies, but it turns out that if people completely avoid looking at you, making eye contact is impossible. I find myself pushing issues closer and closer to people's faces, which perhaps isn't entirely the opposite of *pushy*. The caffeine felt so good mere minutes ago, and now it's like my body is humming at the wrong frequency. Eating would help, but I'm not allowing myself the pizza awaiting us in Mr. Wheeler's room until I've handed out every copy.

Closer to the cafeteria I am desperately staring around, hoping to make someone look at me. It works, but unfortunately the person is Natalie. She smiles and takes a copy of the *Crest* from my outstretched hand.

"I thought distribution was freshman work," she says while flipping through it. "Did you get demoted from editor?"

"Handing out our hard work shouldn't be a low-ranking job," I say. "And, no. Of course I didn't."

"Hmm," she says, still flipping. "Looks like, literally, last week's news. Good luck with that."

"Good luck with short-form journalism that can't report beyond superficialities," I say.

Natalie tosses the paper into the trash can at the entrance to the cafeteria. I walk in, because it's where the largest crowd of people are, and because maybe I'll feel less like this isn't working if my friends are in my sight line.

"Oh my god," says a girl, rushing up to me. "Are those free? Are you giving them out?"

"They are, and I am!" I hand her one, and she shakes her head.

"I need a bunch for my table." She grabs a big chunk of papers and dashes off. My caffeine hum sounds good again, and I think about continuing tradition and—

The girl walks to her lunch table, which turns out to be incredibly wobbly, to the point where beverages look dangerously close to spilling.

But once one of the table legs has a stack of the *Crest* under it, everything's fine.

I carry the remaining papers back to Mr. Wheeler's room and eat the biggest slice of pizza in the box.

CHAPTER FOURTEEN

By evening I can think of little else but tomorrow's first off-campus meeting of the *Crest*, but I don't think that's why suspicion falls over me as I walk into the kitchen before dinner. Darcy's already home, and she and Mom seem to be preparing a large amount of food for three people.

"Is someone coming over?" I ask.

"Just Joe," Darcy says.

There is no *just* Joe! Joe is Mr. Wheeler. Mr. Wheeler should not be in our house less than twenty-four hours before I fully subvert his authority. Mr. Wheeler shouldn't be in our house anyway!

"Ugh," I accidentally say aloud.

"*Jules*," my mothers say together in identical exasperated tones.

"Why can't you guys socialize with him on nights I'm not home?" I ask. "Or wait until after I go to college? It's so awkward."

"He's our neighbor and our friend," Mom says. "And his family's so far away."

"That doesn't mean we have to be his family."

Mr. Wheeler is here before long. He brings a bottle of wine, and my parents coo over it as if he's presenting them with his heir. In return, he acts like the salmon, brown rice, and asparagus have all been personally harvested for him.

The talk is standard for a while: the neighborhood, how everyone's jobs are going, how our rice cooker makes the best rice. And then, as they always do, things take a turn for the horrifying.

"So how's dating, Joe?" Mom leans forward in her chair, as if this is a moment just between them. "Anyone new these days?"

One would think her English-teacher-slash-newspaper-advisor would think about his student in the room and elect to answer the question once she's been excused to her room to complete homework. But, no, never Mr. Wheeler.

"Ha! You guys see me leaving and coming home! Wouldn't you notice if I was somewhere else or someone was here?"

Oh, of course, Mr. Wheeler, we're watching for evidence of your sex life. *Gross.*

"We have someone new at the firm," Darcy says. "I'm going to do some reconnaissance."

"Don't make me any promises, Darcy," Mr. Wheeler says with a chuckle. "So, Jules, are you feeling better about the *Crest*?"

"What's wrong with the *Crest*?" Darcy asks.

"If this is about how you were chosen as editor, honey,

130

you have nothing to feel ashamed about," Mom says. "I know you've put in so much work."

"It's not that big of a deal," I say. "There's now a weekly news series, on the classroom TVs and online."

"That sounds cool," Mom says.

"It is!" Mr. Wheeler says, and I narrow my eyes at him. I don't mean to; they just do it of their own free will. "Jules, you have to admit it's a great program. Natalie came up with the idea and pitched it to Ms. Baugher, who cleared it with administration. It's great seeing a student with so much drive."

Natalie has more drive than I do?

I guess if Natalie invented TALON, convinced a teacher to let her produce it as well as be the host, she has a lot of drive. She potentially out-drives me.

"Like you, Jules," he says, though I'm afraid he's just over-compensating because of my expression. "It's why Jules is one of the best in the class," he tells my parents, and they fall in love with him again. Back to the topic of how such a great guy could be single, but luckily it now feels late enough to excuse myself from the table.

I'm mostly through my homework when Darcy, Mom, and the dogs burst into my room. "What? Is he gone?"

"Be polite, kiddo," Darcy says.

Mom sits down on the bed, between the two dogs. "Do you want to talk about the paper?"

"What's to talk about? The *Crest* was founded the same year the school was, and now *on my watch* it's going to die."

"Jules…" Darcy crowds in next to me and hugs her arms around me. "This isn't about you. Print media's dying all over."

"That doesn't make me feel better."

"It should. It's not because you're doing anything wrong." She picks up the latest issue that's resting on my nightstand. "Look how great this looks."

"The layout's all Carlos, and the cover photos are always by Thatcher."

"You know what she means," Mom says. "We're so proud of you, and if your school news changes, it won't be because of anything you've done wrong."

I pretend to agree with them, but as soon as they leave my room, I get out my red notebook to write down more ideas for our after-after-school meeting.

♥ ♥ ♥

The entire staff behaves for our official staff meeting Tuesday afternoon. No one utters the words *TALON, destruction, the enemy,* or *wartime.*

I only say *dying tradition* once.

We drive over to Carlos's afterward. Anyone with a car chauffeurs anyone without, which means my car is full of freshmen. High school is a crazy time to age us so much. I guess I can believe I once looked so young and tiny, though I don't think I would have asked a senior, *the editor of the school paper I'd just joined*, if she could change the radio from NPR to KIIS FM.

(I do, though. After all, until I was at least fifteen I still occasionally listened to the pop station and therefore heard "Want 2 B Ur Boy" constantly.)

Carlos hasn't let us down on the provided snacks. There are bowls of fruit and a box of pastries from Porto's. I select a bright red apple and eat calmly while everyone crowds around the snacks selection. I want to seem like a true leader, and not someone clawing through a crowd for guava and goat cheese pastries.

"I know we all care about the *Crest*," I say, and even though I thought this was going to be my time, Thatcher stands up next to me. I'm not about to squash his newly revealed competitive streak.

"We all care about killing TALON, at least," he says.

"And it's not worth involving Wheeler," Carlos adds.

"For someone who doesn't seem very with-it," I say, "he's been really fast to shut down important conversations."

Almost everyone laughs at that, and I feel a slight twinge of guilt. Mr. Wheeler might occasionally be smeared with pizza grease, thinks that a frumpy cardigan is professional menswear, and *talks in front of me about his love life*, but—no. If he doesn't care about legacy, he doesn't matter.

"The truth is that people don't seem very interested in the paper anymore," I say. "We printed less this week, and we still had too many left over." I picture the papers tossed into the recycle bins behind the school and shudder.

"So let's get them interested." I take out a portable whiteboard I bought this weekend and set it up. "What are some ideas?"

In my head, this was the moment when everyone's voice would ring out loudly, and I'd frantically scribble every excellent thought until the board was full. By now I really should have learned to stop assuming things would go how they did in my head.

Finally, Marisa speaks up. "What about letting other people get more involved? People love seeing their own face, right? Maybe every week we interview a student or let them have a guest column or both?"

"Great," I say, writing *People like to see their own face!* on the board. "What else?"

"We could poach someone else," Kari Ellison says.

"Someone *else*?" Amanda asks. "I was *poached*?"

I try to come up with something about the grand tradition of bringing the best talent on board from wherever we can, but Carlos speaks before I can.

"Well, yeah," he says with a laugh. "I thought that was pretty obvious. Feel complimented!"

Amazingly, that seems to settle Amanda, as well as Tessa, who looked a little twitchy for a moment.

It takes at least twenty minutes, and the board never fills the way it did in my fantasy, but we eventually have a few ideas.

I'm about to take a vote to see which we should try first when a freshman's hand shoots into the air.

"Um, Julia? Jules? Are you going out with Alex Powell? Because even though he's on TALON, I'm sure people would read an interview with him, and..." Her voice trails off as she notices Carlos, Thatcher, and me staring daggers at her. I know it's not professional to stare daggers at an underling, but it must be more than marginally better than crying.

"I'm not going out with Alex Powell," I say. "For the record. For everyone's records."

"People do want to read about him, though," Marisa says. "Maybe someone could still interview him? Everyone says he's nice."

"He isn't nice," I say. "He's part of TALON. He's *the enemy*. We aren't interviewing him."

"Maybe not an interview," Carlos says. "Maybe some dirt. Why's he here? What's he been up to? Why isn't he famous anymore? Investigative journalism at its finest."

"You're the *layout editor*," I say.

"I'm part of the *Crest* revolution," he says with a grin.

"Hey," Thatcher says. "I'm friends with the guy. I know he's the enemy as far as the *Crest* is concerned, but...let's focus somewhere besides Powell. Okay?"

"Unless there is dirt," I find myself saying. If Alex could betray me so easily, if he could say things just because he knew I wanted to hear them, what else is he capable of? We should all be prepared.

After we vote on which idea we'll take to Mr. Wheeler tomorrow, people start slowly filing out. The carless's parents pull up outside to pick them up. I transfer the whiteboard's list to my red notebook while Thatcher helps Carlos clean up.

"Hey, um," I say as Thatcher walks back into the living room from the kitchen. "I know he's your friend. Sorry if that was…"

Thatcher shrugs. "Can't imagine there's actual dirt on Powell. And I'm sorry for whatever happened, so if you need to let the freshman go on some Chaos 4 All scavenger hunt, be my guest. You need help out to your car?"

"I'm fine; the whiteboard's collapsible, and it came with its own carrying case," I say, and I realize I'm far too enthusiastic about the whiteboard and its capabilities, so I wave good-bye to him and Carlos and take off.

Once I'm home I help Mom with eggplant parmigiana, though Darcy ends up working too late to eat with us. I've never kept secrets from my parents before, but I think they're far too enamored with Mr. Wheeler to support our revolution. Also, perhaps, *revolution* is too strong a word for extra newspaper meetings off-campus that just seem like regular newspaper meetings minus Mr. Wheeler and plus fruits and pastries.

♥ ♥ ♥

Mr. Wheeler, amazingly, likes our guest column idea, and so we have enough time to complete a column introducing the idea and calling for submissions for the next issue of the *Crest*.

When we hand the papers out the next Monday, it's something to tell people as they walk by, and it turns out Marisa is right. People *love* even the *thought* of seeing their own face in black and white. We had a smaller number of issues printed this week, sure, but we hand out almost every single one.

"I feel like I never see you."

I nearly drop my books at the sound of Sadie's voice as I head out of Mr. Wheeler's classroom. "You scared me. And I always spend Monday lunches with the newspaper staff."

"Mondays, sure, but we didn't do anything this weekend, and you didn't even respond to my text on Friday about potential color ideas." Sadie gestures to her electric-blue hair, which is the brightest it's been in a while. "And you haven't said anything about this. Is it bad? Do I look like a Smurf?"

"Smurfs have blue skin, not blue hair," I say. "So, no. Sorry. There's just so much going on with the *Crest*, and I did a bunch of practice SAT sessions and started on my second draft of my admissions essay."

"When you're running the world someday, you'll never have time for me," Sadie says.

"By then you won't care," I say, which makes her eyes widen. But in the future, where will Sadie end up? Somewhere much cooler than me, that's for sure. Right now I'm fairly certain our friendship completes each other, but will it be the same when we're adults? "I didn't mean anything bad."

"There aren't really any good ways to take that," she says. "Dork. What are you doing tonight? I demand we hang out."

"Homework," I say.

"We *all* have homework. You can come over to my house or me to yours, your choice. Or something cooler, like—"

"I have no choice in this, do I?"

"None!" She grins at me before taking off down the hallway. "See you in American lit!"

Something cooler turns out to be a bar on York that doesn't card because they also serve food, so I guess we can technically be inside. Everyone there is in black or denim or leopard print, and every girl besides us seems to have blunt bangs and perfect red lipstick. Sadie stands out because even in the dim light her hair practically glows, and I stand out because I'm wearing navy and pale blue with my blond hair back in a ponytail tied at the height the Internet deems most professional.

"I need my mom to go back to work," she says, playing with the cherry she'd requested for her Diet Coke. It semi-looks like a cocktail now, or at least it did before she started playing with it. "She's home all the time. It's killing my mojo."

"What do you need your mojo for?" I ask.

"Stop being so literal. You know what I mean! There's just always someone around, and she's so up in my business."

I laugh. "That's just what moms do. I should know; I'm a mom expert."

"Having two moms doesn't make you a mom expert!"

"Actually, I think it does."

"Yours aren't always making up for lost time. The great

Paige Sheraton has to prove she loves me even though she worked insane hours for three months."

"Darcy's a *lawyer*. That's exactly what it's like. Sometimes after a big case she asks to check my homework, so that she's familiar with my academic life." I force Sadie to make direct eye contact with me. "She actually says the part about familiarizing herself with my academic life, you realize."

"I need this year to start figuring out my life," Sadie says. "I'm not like you, you realize. I don't have a ten-year plan."

"I have a five-year plan," I say. "Not a ten-year one. Not yet."

"Jules, come on. Do you know how hard it is to figure out what you want to do when Paige Sheraton is around, being all larger than life? Suddenly I can't tell her ideas from my own."

"I really think that's just a mom thing," I say.

"You're terrible at this," she says as a waiter sets down her burger and my salad. "Can't I have some sympathy?"

"I'm sorry, miss, what did you need?" the waiter asks, and we both burst into laughter.

"Sorry, nothing from you," Sadie says through giggles, and the waiter takes off. "What do you think he would have done if I'd actually asked him for some sympathy?"

I smile at her. "Now I'm a little sad you didn't."

CHAPTER FIFTEEN

We fly through our newspaper meeting the next afternoon. When we reconvene at Carlos's, it's so automatic that it's almost as if we've been having double meetings since the beginning of time. In Mr. Wheeler's classroom, he and I are the only ones who stand and address the room, but in Carlos's living room it's me plus Carlos and Thatcher. If Mr. Wheeler had asked me to split editor duties, I'm not sure how I would have managed to agree, but here it just happened. I've decided not to fight it.

"I have an idea that'll blow everyone's minds," says a freshman, which is a pretty bold move for someone who just started. He takes a moment to, I guess, build anticipation. I must admit it works a little. "What if one of us quits and joins TALON?"

"That's what's happening anyway!" I say. "How is that good?"

"No," Thatcher says. "Like a secret agent."

"Exactly," the freshman says. "I'll do it. I volunteer."

"No offense," Carlos says, very gently, "but maybe someone else should be the secret agent."

"Don't I seem like I can be secretive?" the freshman asks. "I've seen all the James Bond movies."

"You're a freshman," I say. "Why would TALON want you? We need a better draw than a freshman with no résumé outside of 007 knowledge."

"Ouch," "Burn," and "*Shiiiiiit*" are the only three things that I hear chorusing around the room.

"I'll do it," Marisa says. "I know Natalie wanted me to join."

"What do you mean?" I ask.

"She asked me," she says.

"Wait, you knew about TALON? Before it happened? Why didn't you say anything?"

"It didn't sound like a big deal," she says. "And I like the *Crest*, and I'm hoping I'll—anyway. I didn't know much about TALON because I wasn't interested in joining. I wasn't keeping anything from anyone."

"Okay," I say. "Join TALON."

"Are you mad?" she asks.

The room murmurs a bunch of noes, most audibly from Carlos and Thatcher. But I know my face lets me down. I'm not sure if it's tradition for the graduating editor to recommend next year's to Mr. Wheeler, but I hope that it is, and I'd been planning on recommending Marisa.

After the meeting's over, I ask Carlos and Thatcher if they want to brainstorm further, but Thatcher's meeting up with

Em, and Carlos is seeing a movie with non-*Crest* friends. As I'm driving home I think I might miss Alex, but that doesn't make any sense. He was only a week and a half of my life, and how does anything that happens in a week and a half make enough of an impression on your life to feel it after it's gone?

♥ ♥ ♥

Marisa's at my locker when I get to school the next morning.

"I know you hate me," she says. "And I don't blame you."

"I don't hate you," I say. "I was just surprised."

"I didn't connect anything," she says. "Natalie didn't give very many details."

"You're a very good journalist," I say. "So actually that's hard for me to believe."

"I take this seriously too." Marisa stares at me. She's only five-foot-even, but it feels like we're making level eye contact. "I wouldn't jeopardize the *Crest*, and honestly it pisses me off that you think I would. You're not the only one who cares, Jules."

"I never said that I am."

"Anyway," she says. "I talked to Natalie this morning, and she said she has to think about it and see what positions are still open."

"Did you say why you were leaving the *Crest*?" I ask. "We should have come up with a cover story for you yesterday."

"I could handle my own cover story, Jules. I'm a junior, not a freshman," she says. "I told her I care about new media. I'll let you know what happens. Okay?"

"Okay. See you in fourth period," I say. "I'm really not mad."

"You really are," she says. "I get it. I'm sure it sucked that almost half the staff followed Natalie."

Obviously, I've known that was true, but it isn't a great thing to hear aloud. Of course I've never been popular, but Eagle Vista isn't the sort of school with jocks and preps and the other divisions that Sadie and I feared based on the movies we watched in middle school. It's never mattered that I don't have legions of admirers, but I guess that if I did, TALON might have gone down differently. Who would leave someone they loved?

"Do you know if she asked all of them?" I ask. There's comfort in knowing people *did* choose me, or at least chose tradition and honor. "The way she asked you?"

Marisa sighs. "How would I know?"

It hits me that even though I've seen her work her butt off for the *Crest*, I don't know Marisa well enough to realize she could be so annoyed at dealing with this. With me.

She walks off before I can say anything else, which is possibly for the best because I might actually be mad at her. I feel something, at least, and it's not just that people wanted to stop working with me—or at least didn't mind. What if I could have seen TALON coming? Why does it feel like someone could have warned me about the way my year would go, but no one thought it mattered enough to tell me?

144

My friends show up, and everyone's in such good moods even though it's morning. Sadie has a whole bag of scones that she's sharing—I guess Paige still isn't filming anything— but I have no appetite, even upon hearing that they have a Meyer lemon glaze. Sadie and Em have the senior year ahead of them that they'd expected. Neither of them have to save a legacy, practically single-handedly.

With a broken heart.

♥ ♥ ♥

I'm on my way to lunch later when Natalie walks right up to me.

"Julia," she says. "Do you think that I'm an idiot?"

"No," I say. "Of course not. Your grades are very good."

"Why would Marisa, who had zero interest in TALON mere weeks ago, suddenly be interested in joining?" she asks with a smirk.

"She cares about new media," I say quickly.

"I saw you two talking earlier," she says. "And as if the only viable candidate for editor next year would move over to TALON."

"You were a viable candidate," I say. "For this year. And you moved over."

"I didn't 'move over,' Julia," she says. "I *founded* TALON. And, anyway, everyone knew you would have pushed your way into that position no matter what, so what was I sticking around for?"

"Who's everyone?" I ask as I realize that maybe I don't want to know.

Natalie smiles as she crosses her arms. "I'll let Marisa know that her less-than-punctual application to TALON has been declined. Good luck with the *Crest*, Julia."

"Good luck with the downfall of respectable journalism," I say. "I'm sure it's exciting being a part of that."

I walk to the cafeteria and sit down at the table even though of course Alex is there. Everyone seems to be talking about a video going around of a baby falling over a cat. I'm in no mood to pull it up on my phone, or even to exert the effort to look at it on Justin's phone. A baby falling over a cat feels like a metaphor for my whole life right now.

"Ugh," Sadie says. "I'm already sick of all our lunch options."

"Live every day like it's Taco Day," Justin says. "Because soon it will be again."

"I don't think it works like that," Em says to him.

"They should let us pick the options," Sadie says. "At least sometimes."

"Oh," I say, and I realize from everyone's expressions that I say it loudly. *Too* loudly. But epiphanies are hard to keep to oneself.

Even an epiphany about lunch specials.

As I start scribbling into my red notebook, I feel eyes on me. Well, everyone is watching me, but I feel specific eyes on me. Alex's gaze is distinctive; I wonder if it always will be.

"Voting for lunch is a good idea," Alex says.

"I don't need your approval," I say as I'm figuring out who we'd have to ask. Is it someone in the cafeteria or much higher up in administration? Would it be a limited choice between existing options or could we ask for more adventurous meals? Maybe we could get local food vendors and restaurants involved.

"Of course not," Alex says. "Whoever pulls it off first would have a lot of people's approval."

His words are a lightning bolt down the center of my heart. TALON is the enemy, obviously, and therefore Alex is the enemy. But never before has Alex acted so... TALON.

"It's my idea," I say.

"You didn't even say it out loud," he says. "You said 'Oh,' really loud, and that was it. I could have come up with it too. Clearly, I *did* come up with it too."

The rest of the lunch table is watching us closely, looking back and forth like we're the most ridiculously over-the-top couple fighting through half of a *Bachelor in Paradise* episode.

I gather my things, because I'm sure Mr. Wheeler is in his office. But Alex gets out his phone and texts casually. I remember when I was the one getting his casually sent lunchtime texts. Are there girls on TALON he thinks are cute? If he liked me because I cared about things, what must he think of Natalie? How could he *not* like Natalie?

"You guys are pretty low-tech," Alex says with a grin. "You should look into texting."

"Obviously we have texting on our phones, Alex, this isn't the late 1990s," I say.

Em and Thatcher are literally leaning forward, resting their chins on their hands, watching us. We've become dinner theater—*lunch theater.*

"Good luck," Alex says, still grinning. I can't believe I ever liked that grin!

"To you too." I walk off to Mr. Wheeler's classroom. He isn't as excited the next day about our voting-for-lunch idea as we are—or, well, *I*, am—but he makes the appropriate calls to administration and gets approval. At our next meeting, Carlos designs a little ballot that will appear in all our issues moving forward. We have to let people select from existing options, so it's not quite as exciting a victory as we'd—*I'd*—seen it, but we still beat TALON to it.

But when we arrive at our fourth-period newspaper class on Friday, two of the freshmen are missing.

CHAPTER SIXTEEN

"Do you think they had them killed?"

Everyone in the room stares at me. For a moment it's everything I dreamed of. I have everyone's rapt attention, even Mr. Wheeler's. I've been ready to command a room like this for as long as I can remember.

But of course then I realize I've just proposed that two of our staff members were murdered. And maybe all this attention isn't because I've finally asked the right question of my staff.

"Jules, sit down," Mr. Wheeler says. "Of course Leah and Max weren't *murdered*. They've decided to join TALON, so we can decide if we want to pull together and work a little harder, or if we want to take a look at the freshman submissions again to see if a couple of them are interested in joining late."

"Mr. Wheeler, isn't that more of a top-level-staff decision?" I ask, and then all eyes are on me again. Yes, we've been doing things in more of a democratic manner in our after-after-school meetings, but there's still an order to things. There *should* be, at least.

"Fine, Jules, we can discuss after school," Mr. Wheeler says with a deep sigh. I probably should have just let it go, because during the after-school meeting, it takes all of two minutes for us to agree that at this point we might as well just work with our existing staff, since we'd already brought back Amanda and brought on Tessa. But policy and procedure mean something, even if I have to remind Mr. Wheeler of that sometimes.

From school I drive to Sadie's, where we're all meeting before we go out. Sadie's dad, Ryan, opens the front door and steps aside for me to walk in. When I was little, the guiltiest I ever felt were the times I wished Ryan was my dad too. He was so tall and funny and... *dadlike.* But I only had to grow up a few years to realize Mom and Darcy are as well matched a set as Ryan and Paige, and just because our families were different didn't mean I was missing out on things.

Em is in the kitchen with Paige, where Paige is showing her an ice-cream maker from Williams-Sonoma. Sadie's at the kitchen table looking at something on her phone.

I really hope it's not the cat/baby video.

"Hey," she says, looking up at me. "Rescue me from hearing about the ideal firmness of ice cream."

I sit down next to her. "Sorry I'm late. After-school meeting."

"We actually figured you'd cancel, so I'm glad you're here at all."

"Why would I cancel?"

"You've just been really preoccupied with the whole news-paper thing."

"It's not a *whole newspaper thing*," I say. "If you didn't know, the *Crest* is a hundred-and-four-year-old tradition, and it's become my responsibility to make sure its legacy doesn't—"

"We know," Em says from across the room. "We're all root-ing for you, Jules."

"This is so annoying," Sadie says, and my heart jumps that she's talking about me. "I organize going out tonight, and Mom still finds a way to make everything about her."

"It's just an ice-cream maker," I say. "People love ice cream."

"It's not enough that she's on-screen, all the time, but she has to get attention even in our own home, where I should stand a fair shot."

"Doughnuts," I say. "I've found they're even more compel-ling than ice cream."

"I'm trying to have a real conversation with you, you know," Sadie says.

"Jules!" Paige calls. "You haven't even said hi to me yet!"

I give Sadie what I hope is an apologetic look before join-ing Paige and Em.

♥ ♥ ♥

I'm not surprised the boys are meeting us at the Los Feliz 3 Cinemas, and I'm not even surprised that, just like lunchtime, "the boys" includes Alex. It would just be far less troubling if everyone else wasn't literally coupled up. I duck into the bookstore next door while everyone else is killing time outside before the movie starts. I'm checking out titles on historic leaders when Sadie pops up right in front of an Abraham Lincoln biography.

"I didn't know he was coming," she says.

"It's okay."

"You can sit on my other side," she says. "We'll make sure he's at the other end."

"Why does he think he can just do this?" I ask softly. "I thought he was nice. Wouldn't someone nice just leave me alone?"

"Well, he doesn't have any other friends," Sadie says with a laugh. "But, I know."

"Boys should disappear when they hurt you."

"Oh my god, I know, right? That's why normally I only recommend dating boys from other schools. Keep your friends close and your boyfriends farther away."

We do follow that mantra during the movie, with me at one end of our row and Alex at the other. I haven't ever been to see a movie with two other couples to my left before, and I'm not sure if it's strange to worry that they'll start making out as soon as the lights go down.

Luckily, that doesn't happen.

I want to get lost in the movie, but I'm too aware of my

friends, of the boys, and of Alex five seats away. I sort out hypothetical scenarios in my head instead of following the on-screen plot. What if Alex had still betrayed me but not specifically in a TALON way? Would it hurt the same? What if TALON still existed, but Alex had nothing to do with it? Would it feel like it does now?

The lights come up, and I realize the credits are rolling. Sadie grins at me and holds up her nearly empty tub of popcorn.

"Want the rest? I won't tell Darcy."

Darcy likes to make a speech about the dangers of movie popcorn butter whenever our families go to the movies, or sometimes even when we merely talk about movies. Considering that Paige and Ryan are *in* movies, this means it comes up a lot.

"She'll smell it on me," I say. "I'd probably get in less trouble for drinking."

Justin leans over so we can see each other around Sadie. "What's the most rebellious thing you've ever done?"

"What are you talking about? I've never done anything rebellious in my life! I'm wearing *a sweater set,* Justin."

"A crazy-stylish sweater set," Sadie says.

Justin wants us to explain sweater sets, and by then Em and Thatcher have decided we should go down the street to Machos Tacos to get food. It's a pretty intimidating taco stand, as they have two grumpy signs hanging right next to the order menu: CHIPS ARE NOT FREE! and YOU WANT EXTRA? NO PROBLEM. PAY EXTRA. Whenever I'm there, I make sure to smile like I'm on liaison duty. You hear that smiling is contagious, but some people must be immune.

"Those signs are really intense," Alex says. If it were anyone else, I'd jump in, because this really is a topic I could discuss for quite a while. But I just silently eat my potato tacos while hoping the boys and girls will separate soon. That doesn't happen, though, because of course girlfriends want to be with their boyfriends and vice versa.

Since I don't want to be a bad friend or seem jealous, I find myself offering to give Alex a ride home. If I don't, I'm not sure how he'll ever get there.

"Thanks," he says, and I wonder if he's also thinking about the fact that last time we were together in my car, we made out. If I close my eyes, I know I could feel his hands on my bare skin. Luckily, since I'm driving, I have no opportunity to close my eyes.

"Congrats on the cafeteria thing," Alex says. "I guess you beat us."

"Congratulations on the freshmen," I say. "I'm sure they've become vital members of TALON."

"Hey," he says. "My congratulations were sincere, not ironic."

"Were they?" I ask.

"Partially," he says after a pause.

"Mine were too. Freshmen work really hard."

Alex laughs, and I force down the corners of my mouth

so I don't smile, even in this dark car. I never knew that you could miss someone even when they're sitting next to you.

Darcy and Mom are watching TV in the living room when I get home, but they turn it off as soon as I close the door. I'm not well acquainted with getting in trouble, but as they watch me from their spots on the sofa, this feels to me like that.

"Did you have fun tonight?" Mom asks.

"Sure," I say, leaning over to pet Peanut and Daisy. "It would have been better if Alex wasn't there, but, it was okay."

"Joe stopped by earlier," Darcy says.

"Ugh," I say without thinking. "Sorry, I meant, 'Oh?' "

"Sit down, kiddo," Darcy says.

"Is everything all right with you?" Mom asks.

I sit down in the cushy leather chair next to the sofa. "What do you mean?"

"We know the editor position means a lot to you," Darcy says. "And we know how hard you worked to get here."

"But, honey, it's just one part of your senior year of high school," Mom says.

"Senior year is an important time," I say. "SATs, Brown admission—"

"Boys," Mom says.

"Your friends," Darcy says.

"I was just out with my friends! And I tried boys; they're awful. I'll wait until college, thank you. Or maybe until I have a decent job after graduate school. You both married women, so I can't believe you're bothering me about boys!"

"I'm sorry that it didn't work out with Alex," Darcy says. "And I'm sorry about this video series. I know that your year isn't going the way you'd hoped that it would."

"Am I in trouble for all of this?" I ask. And then I burst into tears because it's bad enough everything is screwed up for me, but I've disappointed my moms. My moms have done so much for me to simply *exist*, and this is their thanks.

"Get over here," Darcy says, and I crowd onto the sofa between them. The dogs run over and hop up on top of us. We're covered in dogs.

"Of course you aren't in trouble," Darcy says.

"We love that you care about everything so much," Mom says. "But you have to give yourself a break, Jules."

"No one finds victory while giving herself a break."

"Do you hear yourself?" Darcy asks.

"*Yes*. I sound inspiring."

They burst into laughter, and while that isn't what I was going for, it's better than all this concern and disappointment. I change the subject to Paige's ice-cream maker, but I guess that's non-news because both Mom and Darcy already received texts from Paige about it. We discuss getting our own but decide to wait and see if Paige makes us pints and pints of ice cream with no effort on our parts.

I can't believe that next year when I have a not-great Friday I won't be able to hang out on the sofa with my parents. On the plus side, I assume whomever I'm hanging out with in one year won't be nearly as disappointed in me.

♥ ♥ ♥

"I don't want anyone to panic," Mr. Wheeler greets us in fourth period on Monday, which is a pretty guaranteed way to panic a roomful of people. "But we did have a minor act of vandalism over the weekend."

Immediately, there are shouted questions: "Spray painting?" "Did your house get TPed?" "Who got keyed?"

Mr. Wheeler waves his arms around in what I can only assume he thinks is a calming gesture. "It's only the computer keyboards," he says.

Carlos gets up to look. "They're all missing letters. *T, O, A, L—*"

"Let me guess," Thatcher says. "*N?*"

"Toaln?" a freshman asks.

"TALON," says everyone else.

"It's not the smartest vandalism," Mr. Wheeler says, and chuckles. "Obviously I've talked to their advisor, and they'll be replacing the missing keyboards."

"Can't they just put the letters back?" Thatcher asks.

"Not now that they've been disgraced, they can't," I say. "We demand new keyboards."

"Jules, I literally just said that they're replacing the keyboards," Mr. Wheeler says. "For now just figure out how to work around it. Or type your pieces at home."

A folded piece of paper hits my desktop. I haven't been passed a note in ages, not since we all got iPhones, plus there's the long-standing tradition of whispering. So I unfold it slowly and carefully.

WHAT ARE WE STEALING??

I don't like to stereotype, but it does look like girl handwriting. I make eye contact with Marisa, who grins.

Well, obviously nothing that spells "T-H-E C-R-E-S-T"!! I write. *We'll definitely be smarter at vandalism and/or theft!*

Thatcher grabs the note from me. He reads it, grins, and then passes it on to Marisa.

"Marisa, what is that?" Mr. Wheeler asks her. "You guys can talk freely in here, you know—you don't have to pass notes."

"It's nothing." Marisa tucks the note down the front of her shirt. "You can't make me show it to you now."

"I...I wasn't going to make you show me." Mr. Wheeler sighs. "Can we all maybe take a step back? I know you all feel like you have some kind of rivalry with TALON, but can't you see how you guys are all on the same side?"

"We most definitely are not on the same side, Mr. Wheeler," I say. "It's insulting to even say that."

"Guys, there's no need for retaliation," he says. "I want to make it very clear that you're not going to steal anything from TALON, deface any of their property, or anything along those lines. If anything happened right now, it would be pretty obvious who'd done it. Okay?"

We all murmur our agreement, though I'm actually working harder brainstorming vandalizing possibilities than story pitches for this week. All of this delinquent behavior is new to me, and there's no part of it that seems to come naturally.

"Don't worry about it, Jules," Carlos tells me after the bell rings and we're headed out to the hallway. "I've got it handled."

"Do you need my help? What are you doing? It doesn't spell *The Crest*, does it? Is it illegal?"

"I've got it," he says. "Trust me?"

"Just promise me it won't spell *The Crest*, okay?"

"Jules, I'm not an idiot."

I spend the whole week waiting to see what Carlos has planned. At first, every minute where TALON hasn't been publicly vandalized feels like wasted time. But then it begins to seem like the smart choice to wait; a little distance from the dumb and obvious keyboard prank will make us look less like the clear suspects.

On Friday morning, the classroom TV turns on at the usual time for TALON. But Natalie only has a few perfect newscaster-style words out of her mouth before her face cuts out and something else appears.

No, not a butt.

It's Alex's face. Well, technically, it's five faces. It's Chaos 4 All.

"Hey!" the Alex in the video says. He's so small. The size of a freshman. His voice is a little higher too. "We're—"

And then they all yell together "Chaos 4 All!" while leaping into the air in sort of a kung fu way. Then it cuts directly to the "Want 2 B Ur Boy" video. I haven't seen it since that night Sadie and I watched all the videos. At first it felt somehow too personal, as if I'd stumbled on Alex's old diaries and shouldn't have gotten a glimpse. And then once he wasn't mine anymore—*mine?* Jules, oh my god, you didn't *own him.* But once he was out of my life, I didn't want to watch the videos. It hurt too much.

Now, though, it doesn't hurt.

At first, everyone in the classroom just stares at the TV. But someone giggles during the kung fu jumping, and then, well, this is the closest thing to *all hell breaks loose* that I've ever witnessed. Some people gasp when "Want 2 B Ur Boy" starts. More people laugh. A few voices sing along, including Sadie's.

I give her a look.

"What? It's catchy. *Maybe U C all the looks I steal...*"

"Stop it," I say, but more people are singing, and I laugh. Soon, whoever isn't singing is laughing. Even Ms. Cannon, for the moment, doesn't look too annoyed. The song is on the bridge (*Girl, U just don't know how gr8 U R/U R a shooting star*) when the feed cuts out, and somehow it segues seamlessly back into TALON. Natalie's serious face puts every single person over the edge, and I realize Carlos must be to thank for all of this.

160

Oh no. Does that mean last year's butt was Carlos's? It's nothing personal against Carlos. I just don't want to have seen my fellow staff members' butts.

"This is their best episode yet," Sadie says. It's not even a Sadie-style whisper. She just flat-out says it.

"That's enough, Miss Sheraton-Hayes," Ms. Cannon says, but it's with the hint of a smile. "Let's finish this and then get back to Rome."

When the bell rings and everyone floods into the hallways, it's much louder than usual. I spot Alex making his way through, staring straight ahead. He's either ignoring or isn't noticing how many people are staring at him. The general attention paid to Alex has cooled down a lot since his first couple of weeks, but right at this moment, it's reached that level again. Maybe it's even surpassed it.

At lunch he's already at the table when the rest of us arrive with our food. His eyes are focused straight down at the tabletop, even when Justin and Sadie start tossing Skittles back and forth. Em pushes half of her sandwich toward Alex, but he shakes his head. Even Sadie's lunchtime poll (this one is a new question: "Which fruit looks the weirdest?") doesn't get an answer from him. (The rest of the responses are fairly evenly split between star fruit and kiwi, with one vote for dragon fruit.)

I'd feel sorry for Alex if I thought he was someone still deserving any of my nice emotions.

CHAPTER SEVENTEEN

I don't go out on Friday night because our first chance to take the SAT in senior year is first thing on Saturday morning. Of course, I took SATs last year and got great scores, and I've been taking more practice tests since then. There's no reason based off my current scores that getting into Brown shouldn't be a reasonable possibility, but I can always aim for better. Of course, there are also my essay answers, which I've been rewriting whenever I'm caught up on homework and the *Crest* duties, and my letters of recommendation. Mr. Wheeler still owes me his—and considering he's overseen me as a staff member of the *Crest* throughout high school, his seems extremely important—but I've already secured letters from Ms. Guillory and Mr. Cagan, who was my social sciences teacher last year, plus Santiago and Tricia's boss at Stray Rescue. The Brown website's frequently asked questions state that if your counselor and teacher letters are submitted, it's not necessary to send any others unless they show unique knowledge of strengths and skills. But there's nothing I do at school that's like my work with the dogs, so I figure that it can't hurt.

I'd feel settled about all of these facts if not for another one: Brown University takes only 8.6 percent of its applicants. And of course I work hard, all of the time, but so do a lot of people. Just in our school, I know off the top of my head that Natalie, Thatcher, and Carlos work as hard as I do.

So I'm not worried about the test when I show up, because even if I can't raise my scores, I know I'm already in a great place. And maybe because I practiced so much since last year, or even because I've always been decent at taking tests, it goes just like I'd hoped—even more smoothly than last year. My scores are barely on my mind as I finish and leave the school for a later-than-usual shift at Stray Rescue. At some point soon I'll have that final number. And hopefully by then I'll have Mr. Wheeler's recommendation letter—not that I think that'll happen without some hounding on my part. Everything will be lined up and ready to submit online and through the mail.

And then I just wait, for six or seven terrible weeks, until I find out. There are other schools on my backup plan, but I've wanted it to be Brown for as long as I can remember.

Yes, it's Ivy League, and if I'm honest with myself, that means something to me. But at Brown, I'll be responsible for helping to shape my own future. I'll have to design my own undergraduate program—with help from professionals, of course—and I'll make sure everything lines up so that I learn how to lead others and achieve goals. I like that a school as historic and respected as Brown also respects its students that way. I'm ready for more responsibility, and to carve out the tracks toward the future I'll have.

Last year, Mom and Darcy took me to Rhode Island to tour the campus, which was a big deal not just because it was Brown, but because we don't get to take a lot of family trips thanks to Darcy's job. They stayed at a bed-and-breakfast they still occasionally rhapsodize over (apparently the brunch was superb), but I got to stay on campus, in a sleeping bag on a dorm-room floor.

In some ways, being on campus reminded me a lot of being home. The girl who hosted me, her roommate, and their friends seemed fun and laid-back in a way that wasn't so different from my group of friends. They'd earned it, though; they'd already achieved so much by being there. And our conversations weren't about weird fruits or which sodas were the worst. We talked about life and our futures and the kinds of change we hoped to see in the world. Now, of course, it sounds cheesy, looking back on it, but I have a feeling that Brown is the kind of place where I can give rousing speeches and get away with it.

♥ ♥ ♥

On Monday, Mr. Wheeler doesn't say a word about "Want 2 B Ur Boy" during fourth period. Tuesday's class passes without incident too. At this point, more than a full week has passed since the keyboards incident, and more than a full weekend since the boy-band one. It makes sense that we're in the clear. If this were another teacher, every moment since Natalie's face cut into Alex's singing might be packed with the scariest type of anticipation. But Mr. Wheeler and I walked by each other several times over the weekend in the neighborhood, and I didn't even feel mildly nervous.

"So, guys," he says once everyone has arrived for our Tuesday after-school meeting, "let's talk about what happened Friday."

I do my best not to look guiltily around the room. Has Carlos concocted a cover story? Technically we've never discussed the specifics, and outside of him assuring me that retribution would be taken care of, I have no details. I have no proof. It's almost as if I could claim ignorance to the whole matter.

Almost.

"What happened Friday?" Marisa asks in a very good innocent tone. I make a mental note to work on cultivating one myself.

"Let's cut out the shenanigans, guys," he says. "I waited until after school so we could discuss this freely."

"Discuss what freely, Mr. Wheeler?" Carlos asks. His innocent voice is far more sarcastic than Marisa's, and I worry the whole operation's going down.

"Never mind." Mr. Wheeler shakes his head. "I hope someday you guys all look back on this and see how silly you were

166

being. There are so many great ways to use your time and efforts and brains!"

"I think the *Crest* is a great use of our time, efforts, and brains," I say, and even though I was striving for *sincere,* my voice rings out with just a little sarcasm. People laugh, so I'm a little glad it happened. Maybe more than a little.

"Everyone, just get to work," he says. "Jules, come on up."

I take over to organize this week's stories and photography assignments, and already it feels like a regular week again. Everyone snaps into action because, TALON or no TALON, we're professionals.

We run out of printer paper while we're passing around student submissions for the guest column, and since I don't think it's fair for a leader to escape all administrative duties, I volunteer to get a new box.

The light's on in the supply room when I walk in. It isn't a surprise, because other groups need things in here too. But the fact that the other person is Alex, well, that part's a surprise.

It isn't just that I've hated all the surprises this year: Natalie's departure from the *Crest*, TALON, and Alex. I've never been a fan of surprises. On my tenth birthday, we went over to Sadie's for what I was told was just a regular dinner, and everyone I knew leaped out of the dark and yelled *Surprise!*

I spent the next hour of the party curled up on Sadie's bed between my parents. Crying.

"Hi," Alex says. "I'll get out of your way as soon as I can. Okay?"

"Okay," I say, and lean against the wall while he collects dry-erase markers from a bin. Whoever orders the markers dumps all of them in one plastic bin, so you have to be really careful you're grabbing something erasable, and not a permanent Sharpie or a highlighter. I can tell Alex hasn't been informed of the dangers of this bin. Obviously many of my goals this year revolve around TALON's destruction, but I don't mean *their whiteboards*. So I step over to help him.

Our hands keep accidentally touching as we're digging through the bin. I laugh to myself that if this were a movie, we'd start making out. But then my fingers entwine with his while we're after the same red Expo marker, and fingers entwining is basically holding hands, and then—oh my god. It *is* like a silly movie because then we *are* making out.

"I missed this so much," I say, of course, because when have I managed to keep a thought from Alex once kissing's involved?

He reaches past me to lock the supply room door, and I take advantage of how close and overlapping our bodies are to pull him back toward me. It's a move I seem to have borrowed from a slick sophisticated movie character.

I don't move to kiss Alex immediately, because I just want to look at him while he's so near to me. Everything's the same, of course. His brown eyes radiate gold in their magical way,

168

he's gotten a haircut, but that wavy lock still flops down perfectly, and I'm convinced, the longer I know him, that I will eventually be able to read his mind via his eyebrows. His eyebrows are everything.

Jules, don't say "Your eyebrows are everything" aloud in this moment of weakness.

"Do you know when I knew I liked you?" Alex slides his hands down my sides, holding me where my waist curves in. "My first day. When your skirt got stuck in the door."

"Oh my god." I close my eyes and shake my head. "I felt like such an idiot."

"You made this amazing face," he says. "Also you had, like…" He laughs softly. "Crazy underwear. I thought, there's more to this girl."

"Oh my god, Alex!" I laugh against his chest. I haven't touched him in weeks, but it's like he's all mine, again, already, immediately. "My *mom* bought me those."

"You're ruining my fantasy," he says, but I don't think that's true because he kisses me again. I hold his face in my hands because it's hard to believe he's real and that this is happening. In the movie of this moment, he'd be a close-up on the screen. On-screen for TALON he's this bold and brave guy, but inches away from me he's just *Alex*, and in the movie I'm imagining now he's just Alex too.

"How much time has gone by?" I ask. "I completely forgot that I came in here for a reason."

"A good reason," he says with a grin.

"Stop being cute," I say. "I have to bring paper back to my staff."

"Your staff," he murmurs in my ear. "You're really powerful."

I don't *decide* that the printer paper can wait, but I do wrap my arms around Alex's shoulders again. I kiss his forehead and I kiss his cheeks and I kiss his lips over and over and over. I try to make up for lost time, kissing for all the days we didn't. A montage plays in my head, all the moments without Alex that now I wish that I'd been kissing him again.

"I have to go," I say once the montage has ended and there's, somehow, a break in the kissing.

"Your staff," he says.

"They really are my staff," I say, and he pulls me close, not into another kiss but a hug. I hug back with everything I have.

"What are you doing after your meeting?" he says.

"I have another—I have something else." Oh my god, a few minutes of kissing and I'm ready to give away all of the *Crest*'s secrets. I'd never make it during wartime if captured by the enemy.

"After that?" he asks.

"I don't know," I say. "Can I text you? Can you drive yet?"

"You can text me," he says, "but, no. I can't drive yet. You'll have to come get me."

His voice sounds warm and husky on *come get me*, and I can't help myself. I'm not sure how I'll ever actually stop kissing him and leave this room.

"Alex?" Someone pounds on the door. "Are you getting thrown by the Sharpies? Someone should have warned you!"

"I'm good!" he calls, then drops his voice. "Text me later, when you're done doing what you're doing."

I hide in the corner until Alex is out of the room, and then wait a few moments before leaving the supply room. I try to rush back toward Mr. Wheeler's classroom without looking like I'm rushing, even though there's no one around.

Until there is.

"Hello, Julia." If I hadn't been focusing on the perfect non-rushing speed, maybe I would have noticed Natalie appearing seemingly out of nowhere. "I'm sure you're very proud of yourself."

"For—" I cut myself off, even though it was on the tip of my tongue to say, *For kissing Alex?* "Wait, for what?"

"For your little broadcast interference," she says. "Targeting one of our staffers."

"I had nothing to do with that," I say as I remember what Mr. Wheeler was lecturing us about today. I think about Alex's face on Friday and worry that he's still wounded, but then it morphs into his close-up face from only minutes ago. I feel myself smiling with no chance of holding it back. Alex couldn't mind too much if what just happened just happened.

"You look very guilty," Natalie says, which is true, just not of what she's thinking. "We aren't idiots."

"How did you know that I was in the hallway?" I ask,

because even though I don't think Alex would use me, the timing is suspicious.

"I was on my way to the restroom," she says. "I'm hardly *stalking you*, Julia. There's no one on TALON who would find that worth the effort. While your 'team' "—she uses air quotes—"spends their time and energy trying to keep us from being seen, it isn't as if the student body and beyond can't watch the entire extended broadcast on VidLook."

"Really?" I ask, trying to adopt an innocent tone. "Because someone thought it was 'worth the effort' "—I use air quotes too—"to vandalize our keyboards, and that seems like it would take more time, energy, and planning than following me in the hallway."

"It's a pretty cheap tactic to attack the personal life of one of our staffers," she continues as if I haven't spoken. "Of course a boy band is easy to laugh at, but Alex achieved a great deal at a young age. That's hardly comedy."

"I didn't say that it was. Or that it's probably an even cheaper tactic to destroy school property, considering that now school funds have to be diverted to replacing keyboards instead of something your brand-new team probably needs."

Marisa walks up to us. "Mr. Wheeler sent me out to find you, Jules. Is everything okay?"

"Everything's fine," I say. "Natalie just wanted to lecture me about what comedy is and isn't."

"That doesn't seem like it would be in Natalie's wheelhouse," Marisa says.

"There's plenty in my wheelhouse," Natalie says. "It's very extensive."

"We don't really have time to hear about your big wheelhouse," I say. "We have important work to do."

Marisa and I walk back to Mr. Wheeler's classroom, which is when it hits me how long I've been gone. "Sorry, it took a while."

"What took a while?" Mr. Wheeler asks. "Where's the paper?"

"Why are you all red?" Carlos asks.

"Natalie intercepted her," Marisa says. "But are they out of paper? There's another stash in the admin office. Since I'm an aide, I can get some."

"Sure," I say, letting Marisa run to another building because I was too distracted to do my job.

"I forgot to say why I'm red," I blurt out, as I try to come up with something reasonable. "I was just looking for paper so long. And getting stressed out. And that room gets warm."

Somehow the meeting ends, and then I'm in my car with freshmen, driving to Carlos's. My phone is lit up with texts when I walk into the second meeting, and I'm afraid they'll all be from Sadie or Mom or Darcy. Maybe Mr. Wheeler figured out that there was paper in the main supply room and I'll get a lecture via text message about wasting student resources. I'm not sure that Mr. Wheeler has my phone number, but it seems possible.

I deleted Alex's number from my phone in what felt like a satisfying moment of closure, but I recognize these digits displayed repeatedly across my screen. These numbers might as well spell out *A-L-E-X* in their own special language.

That was fun.

I missed you.

Somehow still managed to accidentally take a bunch of Sharpies and screwed up our board. You're distracting.

"Jules?"

I look up from my phone to see that everyone but Carlos and Thatcher is already seated, with snacks, and I'm standing facing the wrong direction in an odd corner of the room. How did I even get here?

"How did you guys do it?" a freshman asks.

"Can we hack into the TVs every week?" a sophomore asks.

"Natalie was *pissed*," says Ana Rios.

"There's no proof any of us did anything," Carlos says with the ease of someone who hacks into school closed-circuit TV networks all the time.

"Let's get to work," Thatcher says.

"Yes," I say, even though considering the events of this afternoon, I can barely remember what *work* is.

"Do we wait for their next move?" a freshman asks.

"No," Thatcher says. "Remember, guys, this is war."

"*Real war*," Carlos adds.

"At first we just had to worry about getting up our readership," Thatcher says. "But between the lunch poll and the guest column, we've done that. So now we need to take those guys down harder."

I let Thatcher talk while I think about the phone in my hand and the messages it holds for me. But, actually—

"It isn't just about shutting them down," I point out. "People still aren't reading the paper as much as they were last year. There's still a good chance the *Crest* could lose funding for next year. The closest thing Eagle Vista Academy could have to journalism is watching Kevin point to the historic Trader Joe's sign."

Most of the room seems to murmur what I'm taking as agreement.

"Fine, fine," Thatcher says, but he smiles. "Let's get back to it, then. Jules?"

As I talk I press my thumb to my phone's power button. The room feels, figuratively, like mine again. "Natalie confronted me about the broadcast hack last week, but then she tried to act as if it didn't even matter. She says people could watch the uninterrupted program on VidLook, as if that's actually happening."

We laugh about that for a bit, while Carlos pulls up TALON's VidLook channel so we can laugh at their pathetic numbers. But the numbers aren't pathetic. The numbers aren't going to break any records, but maybe in one of those really specific categories such as *Southern California Private High Schools* they actually could. There are comments too, and not just the type you're used to finding on VidLook, where people suddenly have unrelated things to say about body parts and fluids. There are real comments, and the usernames appear to be from real students.

The numbers and the comments take something out of us, and I find myself packing up my things and then shepherding the freshmen home. I drive myself home without checking in on Alex, considering that I seem to function more rationally when he isn't in the picture. Mom and I make homemade pasta, and Darcy's home on time, and I get through the whole meal with my phone still switched off. Without my phone, Alex might as well not even exist.

Everything would honestly be better if Alex didn't exist.

Actually, it's fine that he exists. But my life would be so much *easier* if he'd never come to our school. And of course that would mean I never would kiss him, that my lips would never feel chapped just from kissing him for a few minutes in a supply room, that we wouldn't have sessions of kissing that feel torn from the screens of romantic comedies, but that would probably be for the best.

I think so, at least.

Mom and Darcy ask if I'm okay, and I don't even know how to respond. I retreat into my room to do my homework, but I end up sitting down with my computer instead. I Google "secret relationship" but it's not as relevant to my life as I want it to be. So I Google "taking down your new media competition" and every article is about a newspaper that goes out of business or turns into a blog, so I give up on Google and get back to homework instead.

CHAPTER EIGHTEEN

When I open my locker the next morning, a scrap of paper falls out and onto my feet. If TALON is up to its flyering again, that can't be good for any of us.

It's not a TALON flyer, though. It's a note.

I'm pretty sure I didn't imagine yesterday. What's up?

I take out my phone and hit the power button. But before it's fully back on, Sadie's at my side.

"I'm glad you're still alive," she says. "I couldn't handle it if you weren't, Jules."

"Are you all right?" I ask.

"You didn't respond to any of my texts last night," she says. "So then I called you, but it went straight to your voice mail. So then I emailed you, like a Luddite!"

"My phone died," I say. "And I didn't notice until just now. Is everything okay?"

"Oh my god, Mom said the most horrible thing to me last night," Sadie says as we walk to women's history. " 'Since

Sadie'll be in New York next year for school, I should *strongly consider* doing a play again. It was always just so far away, but...' *She's following me across the whole freaking country.*"

"She's not following you," I say. "She'll just be there. Working. She won't move into your dorm room with you."

"We'll have to have dinner all the time with my grandma," she says.

"That sounds nice," I say, because I hardly get to see the one of mine who's still alive.

"Jules, *my grandma is so annoying*!" Sadie shakes her head. "And the press will be so excited that the great Paige Sheraton is back on Broadway that she'll have even more attention than usual."

"I'm...sorry?"

"I'm trying so freaking hard to have my own things," Sadie says. "And it feels like Mom gets to all of them before I can."

"I feel like NYU and Broadway will be very separate things," I say.

"You never share my pain." Sadie sits down at her desk. "I hope you at least felt bad when you saw all my missed texts and voice mails."

I still haven't actually looked at my phone since it powered on and I tossed it into my purse. And I'm not sure when I'll get a chance to without an audience, but I take a chance at my locker after first period lets out. I need to grab my books and go, but instead I sort through Sadie's texts just so they don't display as new anymore and check for more texts from Alex.

There's just one more, but I hate seeing it in black and white on my phone: **Are you ignoring me? Everything cool?**

I start typing out that it scares me how quickly I can forget about everything else when he's in the picture, and how kissing him made me so immediately forget about betrayal, and also that there is no way we could publicly be together again after everything that's happening between TALON and the *Crest*. But the text is getting long—and frighteningly intense—so I delete all that and type two words instead.

Everything's cool.

When we sit down at the lunch table, there's—well, hopefully—no indication of yesterday's supply room incident. I try to remain chilly in demeanor in his direction, and he's definitely not trying to include me in any of the weird boy conversations. But, under the table, he rests his foot against mine, so my two-word text must have done its job.

Later at Stray Rescue, we act like barely speaking dog-walking professionals when we arrive, separately, at the shelter. I worry our routine will lose some of its viciousness, so I step up my determination that I'll walk more dogs than ever before. Alex, of course, notices, and soon we're neck and neck.

But then our shifts end, and we head outside, where my car awaits.

"No doughnuts?" Alex asks with a grin as I pull him toward my car.

"Doughnuts later," I say.

We have our old routine ready. Alex pushes back the passenger-side seat and pulls me over to his side. We somehow fit together perfectly; everything feels entwined and our faces are in perfect kissing range. It's hard to imagine I lived without this for weeks.

"Did you have a lot of groupies?" I ask Alex when things have slowed down but we're still curled together on his side of the car. "Before?"

"I...guess?" He laughs. "A lot of them were, like, twelve. But, sure, there were some."

"Some non-twelve-year-olds," I say.

"Yeah. And girlfriends," he says. "Those too."

"You're the first boy I've really liked," I confess. "Except for this annoying boy at gifted camp, but he barely counts."

"Whoa." Alex grins, the grin that melts all my reasonable sense. "I have to hear everything about gifted camp."

"It wasn't a big deal," I say. "It was at a college in Northern California. We lived in the dorms for two weeks and took classes during the day and had normal camp activities in the evenings."

"Like s'mores?" Alex asks.

"Well, it was on a campus. So less outdoorsy, more... three-legged races and everything. I was taller than most of the girls, so no one ever wanted to pair up with me for that."

"I'd pair up with you," Alex says.

"Boys and girls weren't allowed to pair up, Alex," I say.

"Anyway, that was the last time I thought a boy was…" Out loud it feels like such a big confession. Alex has had fans and groupies and girlfriends and sex. I've had one kiss at gifted camp.

"I missed how much you blush," Alex says.

"That's the worst thing about me!"

"Nah." He grins some more. "Doughnuts?"

"You're obsessed with doughnuts," I say.

"So are you." He touches my mouth with his so softly it feels more like a whisper than a kiss. "At school you eat healthier than anyone at our table. And then the second you're through with the dogs…"

I laugh. "Not the *very* second."

♥ ♥ ♥

I thought I'd have to have a delicately worded conversation with Alex about the secrecy we require, but there are too many notes in lockers and foot touches under tables to mistake his intentions for *public*. We don't even text during school hours.

We do text once school's out for the day, but I have Associated Student Body, and by the time I'm out, Alex has to help his mom with chores. Anyway, I have a huge stack of homework as well as student submissions for the *Crest*. We don't even have our next idea for increasing readership, and I don't want to lose momentum on real goals just because the TV-hacking incident felt so successful.

Oh my god, the TV-hacking incident! Should I apologize to Alex? Should I explain I didn't really have anything to do with it? It doesn't seem fair to give up Carlos, or even the *Crest*, but can I spend so much time kissing someone while my organization plots his organization's downfall?

I could really use secret-relationship guidance.

CHAPTER NINETEEN

"Do you want to go out?"

Our Saturday shifts have just ended at Stray Rescue. I'm positive Santiago doesn't know we're back together because he gave me an empathetic little glance as Alex arrived. We managed to pull this off last night too, so much so that when Sadie and I were in the bathroom of Oinkster at the same time, she apologized for Alex being around so much.

"Yes," I reply to Alex. "But somewhere people won't see us."

He laughs. "I'll try not to take that personally. And is that possible?"

"People we know, I mean," I say. "Not people in general."

"My parents are home right now," he says. "Or I'd tell you to come over."

"Oh, you'd *tell* me?" I smile and slip my hand into his. We're standing outside, where theoretically anyone could see us. The moment is full of so much more illicit danger than I ever thought I'd experience.

"I'd *ask* you," he says.

I decide to drive us to Old Town Pasadena. It's only one city over from either here or from Eagle Rock, but when people from school want to hang out, they don't head away from LA proper. If I were Sadie, I'd probably know something cooler to do than hang out in and around shops and restaurants built into old and historic buildings, but even with a secret relationship, I'm not cool.

"How'd your SATs go?" Alex asks me while we're waiting in the long line stretching out the door of 21 Choices, which has twenty-one different ice-cream options every single day. Normally I don't think that it's worth the wait, but today the wait involves holding Alex's hand in the sunshine.

"How did you know I took them?" I ask.

"You mentioned a while back you were going the first week they were available," he says. "Hey, I pay attention."

I smile. "Good! And they were fine. When are you going?"

"Soon," he says. "I guess. I don't know where I want to go to college or what I want to study or…anything in that whole area. Which I guess I should deal with at some point."

"Twenty to fifty percent of college freshmen are undecided," I say. "So you can just pick a good school."

"Everything sounds so simple when Jules McAllister-Morgan declares it," he says with a grin. "Why are you so set on Brown?"

"Oh my god, basically everything. They really emphasize learning for learning's sake, not just to get good grades or

have a good résumé later. You get to design your own program, but since it's Ivy League, I know I can't go too off
course, and I know my degree will be taken seriously after
I graduate. And their campus is beautiful, and when I vis-
ited…" I shrug. "It *felt right*."

"You'll get in," he says.

"Don't jinx it," I say. "But thanks."

My phone beeps in my purse, and I take it out in case it's
one of my moms or anything else that's urgent.

What are you doing?? is lit up on my screen. The message
is from Sadie. It could mean anything. Well, it could mean
two things. Obviously she could want to know if I'm free so we
can do something. But also maybe somehow she knows where
I am and with whom.

"What's up?" Alex asks.

"Nothing," I say as I type back an answer. **Just running
errands after Stray Rescue.** "Alex…I know I probably
shouldn't mention this. But I didn't have anything to do with
your video last week."

He shrugs as we finally step from the outdoors into the
shop. We're so close to ice cream now. "It's okay if you did."

"Okay, but I really didn't."

We step up to order. Alex gets peanut butter brownie, and
I get mango sunshine, which Alex apparently thinks is the
funniest sorbet name he's ever heard, based on his laughter
when I order, at least. Once we've paid, we exit and hunt down
an open bench. We can't hold hands while eating ice-cream

cones, but sitting side by side, I still feel like I'm in another scene straight out of a romantic comedy.

"I know I was supposed to be embarrassed when it happened," Alex says. "Yeah, everyone staring kind of sucks. But I liked being in Chaos 4 All. I'm not saying I want to be again, and it was weird, for sure. But it was cool too."

"You were good," I say. "*Great*, I mean! I'm glad that it was cool."

"I thought I'd get to do it forever," he says. "Back then, at least. It felt like we were the biggest thing in the world. I thought my dad could quit his job and not be gone all the time."

I like the small moments where Alex doesn't sound full of the confidence the world gave him a couple of years ago. On-screen for TALON he has all of it back. Maybe cameras hold all his old magic, so when he's filmed it's like it never went away. But Alex is this guy too, who isn't about to throw a wink to an adoring crowd.

I like both Alexes.

Alex leans over and kisses me. Our lips are sticky and sweet, like Popsicles in summer.

"That was a real ray of mango sunshine," he says, and I laugh so hard I accidentally snort. That sets him off, and then we're both laughing too hard for kissing or for ice-cream cones. I never would have known before Alex that laughing with a boy could sometimes feel just as perfect as kissing one, if he's the right boy.

I guess technically Alex is the wrong boy, but I'm pretending for now that that isn't true.

♥ ♥ ♥

When I drop off Alex at his house, it hits me that I haven't looked at my phone in a couple of hours. Have I ever not looked at my phone for a couple of hours, except to sleep? Alex and I wandered in and out of shops, took photos with Alex's phone in front of City Hall where they shoot TV shows, and snacked at more places than I could ever deem healthy. We barely stopped holding hands. It felt like a real, actual, perfect date.

It felt like how I thought falling in love might feel.

But that all disappears the moment I see my screen full of messages, mostly from Sadie.

Today sucks, call me?
Are you still running errands?
Are you ignoring me?
OH MY GOD ARE YOU SERIOUSLY IGNORING ME?
Jules! Are you OK???

And then a message from Mom:

Is everything okay? Sadie called to see if you were with me. Which you aren't. Text or call me or Darcy so we know you're alive.

I start to text Mom, then I think I should respond to Sadie first, and then I realize the best move is probably to just drive home. Luckily Mom and Darcy are both there, and—even luckier—they only look slightly relieved to see me. Peanut and Daisy, on the other hand, circle around me as if I've been gone for a decade.

"My phone died," I say as I sit down to pet the dogs. "I just plugged it in in the car and saw your message. I'm sorry."

"We aren't that strict," Darcy says. "But we need to know if you won't be home."

"I know," I say.

"Is everything okay?" Mom asks.

"I...made up with Alex," I say, because it sounds like the best way to phrase it. I'm not sure if I can say that we're together again when in public we can't be.

"Oh," Darcy says. "Well, we don't mind if you're out with Alex, and there probably isn't much we wouldn't let you do."

"No!" I say. It might have come out as a yell. "I mean, yes, I was out with Alex, but we just went to Old Town."

"Regardless," she says with an eyebrow arched, "please just let us know you'll be out. And if one of us texts or calls, respond."

"Okay?" Mom asks.

"Of course. I'm sorry. I screwed up. Can I go call Sadie?"

They dismiss me, and I run upstairs—flanked by the dogs—to my room. Sadie's phone goes right to voice mail when I call, so I text. Sorry. My phone died. Are you okay?

There's a long pause before I can see that she's typing back. I'm fine. I'm out with Em. See you Monday.

I guess that sometimes Sadie or I go out with only Em, when the other is busy, or out of town, or sick. But I'm not sure I've ever just not been invited. It's fair, since I was unreachable, but I'm reachable now.

CHAPTER TWENTY

As usual, on Monday I'm the one to open the boxes of fresh copies of the *Crest*. This is one of my favorite parts of the week.

But as I'm flipping through, I see something unfamiliar. "There's a printing error! Check all the copies! I repeat, check all the copies!"

"Jules, calm down for a moment." Mr. Wheeler walks up behind me and takes another copy. "Everything looks fine to me."

"That's not a printing error," Carlos says while looking over my shoulder. "That's layout tampering."

"But we saw the proofs on Friday! We approved them on Friday! They were fine on Friday!"

"Jules, *please*."

Ms. Wang, who teaches creative writing in the next classroom, leans into the room. "Is everything okay in here? We heard a lot of yelling."

"Things are fine," Mr. Wheeler says as other staff members

crowd around me. The headline to the guest post for the week isn't "Why I Love the E.V.A. Library," which is what we approved for the issue, but "New Media Is Our Future."

And the guest writer's photo is Natalie's incredibly sleek head shot.

I have two questions immediately: First, how did this get into the paper, and, second, do I need head shots?

"We didn't approve this," I say. "This was supposed to be that piece on the library."

"Natalie's such a good writer," Marisa says, softly, but I hear her. After scanning the first few sentences of the piece, I can't deny this truth, though of course that isn't the point.

"Oh, geez," Mr. Wheeler says, because apparently it's taken him a bit longer than the rest of us to realize this is TALON's doing. "Could you guys all knock this off? I thought we were past this."

"We didn't do anything!" I say.

"Yelling, Jules," Thatcher says softly.

I adjust my tone. "Mr. Wheeler, this was their doing and not ours. Obviously. We wouldn't disgrace our own paper with their biased viewpoint."

"Well…" Mr. Wheeler looks over Natalie's article. "It's a good essay. No one sneaked in anything about butts, ha-ha! Don't worry about it, guys."

"How did they even do this?" Carlos asks.

"They must know someone at the printers," Thatcher says. "They've got a man on the inside."

A whimpering sound erupts from somewhere in the crowd.

"*You?*" Amanda shrieks.

"I'm sorry," Tessa says through tears. "I'm so sorry. Natalie promised me—"

"What?" I ask. "What did she promise?"

Tessa's now crying so hard she can't answer. Amanda talks to her quietly for a few moments.

"Natalie said she'd do everything in her power to get Tessa on air next year," Amanda says. "And also you never published her eagle essay or pushed to have the school adopt a real live eagle."

"That was *never* going to happen!"

"Anyway," Amanda continues, "Tessa got the files to someone at TALON. And they overrode what was in the system somehow."

"Well, it's not that locked down of a system," Mr. Wheeler says, very casually if you ask me. "Let's get to work. Tessa, why don't you take a break and join us when you're feeling up for it."

"We need to discuss this further," I say. "Including disciplinary actions—"

"Jules, that's for me to deal with," Mr. Wheeler says. "For now, let's worry about next week's issue."

We begin outlining the next issue instead of dealing with the situation. Once the bell rings, the freshmen minus Tessa head out to distribute the paper, and the rest of us wait for the pizza to show up. Mr. Wheeler calls me over to his desk, a few feet away from the rest of the staff, and I work on keeping my face set in a non-panicked expression.

"What do you need?" I ask.

"Jules, one reason I selected you as editor this year is your leadership ability," he says. "The other students, especially the freshmen and sophomores, really look up to you in this room. So I need you to calm down and keep things in perspective, okay?"

"*Keep things in perspective?*" I pause and lower my voice because now people are looking. "Mr. Wheeler, Natalie bribed a staffer and sneaked unauthorized material into our publication. I don't think I'm angry enough."

"Jules, you're plenty angry," he says. "These guys wouldn't be so riled up if you took it down a notch or two. That's all I'm asking. Be a good role model."

"Mr. Wheeler, I think that someone who cares passionately *is* a good role model."

He sighs. "There's a line between caring passionately and maybe going a little too far. Can you think hard about what side of the line you're on?"

I feel that we have very different feelings about this figurative line, so I don't say anything. The last thing I need is for him to report in again to Darcy and Mom about how I'm taking this too seriously. So I manage a smile.

The intercom buzzes. "Mr. Wheeler, your pizzas have arrived. We've sent them down to your classroom."

"Jules?" Mr. Wheeler says. "Everything understood?"

"I, um, I hate to bother you," I say, which isn't true but feels like the polite way to check in. "But you said you'd write a letter of—"

"*Yes*," he says as the pizzas arrive. I'm afraid he'll forget we're in the middle of this conversation, but after he pays the delivery people, he grabs a slice of pizza and sits back at his desk facing me.

"Jules, I'm happy to write your letter of recommendation, and I'm working on it. I promise I'll send it in time. You don't have anything to worry about."

"I'm trying to get into Brown," I say. "I have *everything* to worry about."

He chuckles. "Jules, you stress me out on your behalf. Go get a piece of pizza, okay? This is your senior year. You're supposed to have fun."

"That's not what your senior year is for; I can have fun later," I say. "I will get a piece of pizza, though."

♥ ♥ ♥

There's a note in my locker before last period. Handwriting is so much more personal than words on a screen.

Since you missed lunch, can we hang out later?

I manage to smile at him when I walk into American lit. Sadie's not in the room yet, so it feels safe to have just a moment.

"Yes?" he asks.

I have homework, of course, but I find myself making a

tiny nod, just as Sadie walks in. I take my seat as if the conversation never happened. Sadie and I have actually barely talked today, as she arrived in women's history right as the bell rang, and I was in Mr. Wheeler's room during lunch. All of that's normal for a Monday, but after Saturday I'm not sure if everything is okay.

"I'm sorry about my phone," I say, though I've read multiple times that you shouldn't remind people of your past failings by apologizing too frequently or even at all.

"It's fine," Sadie says without looking at me.

"I was irresponsible with charging," I say.

"Phone-charging responsibility is very important, Jules. Everyone knows that." She takes her usual seat next to me, though there still isn't much eye contact. "Did you see Deadline today?"

"I don't really keep up with Hollywood news during class," I say. "So, no. Why?"

"Guess who's in that new movie trilogy based on those dragon books?"

"I have no idea."

"*My mom.* My mom has a job again! She'll be getting out of the house! She's even going on location for a few weeks."

"Congratulations?"

"My life will be so much easier, trust me."

"Your mom's great," I say.

"Great, but a lot to deal with," she says. "And I keep telling you that."

"I just know your parents really well," I say. "That's all."

Sadie sighs. "Probably not as well as I do."

Alex leans forward in his desk as Mr. Wheeler begins his *observing the classroom* attendance taking. "Have you guys read those dragon books? They're actually pretty good."

"Alex, you know you don't get to be in our private conversations anymore," Sadie says to him, and I realize that for a few moments it slipped my mind to pretend to hate him.

Alex glances back and forth between Sadie and me, and I try to explain with a look that Sadie doesn't know. Shouldn't he *just know*, though?

After school I drive to Alex's and wait, parked on his block, for his mom to bring him home. There's something about waiting in a parked car that reminds me of illicit affairs, and I wonder if what's going on counts as an affair. Am I having one? It might at least count as illicit.

Alex walks up to the car and knocks on my window.

"Hi," I say, letting him into the car. He leans in and presses his lips to mine, and in this moment I feel the whole day we couldn't share with each other. "I can't believe you tried to talk to us in American lit."

"I got distracted," he says.

I laugh. "By dragon books?"

Alex sets his hand on my bare knee and squeezes just a little. "By your skirt. And also dragon books. But...also I figured that Sadie knew. Aren't you guys best friends? I thought you told each other everything."

"Alex, we're at war," I say. "If anyone knew...I thought you understood that."

He's silent a moment, but then he laughs. "I missed all your declarations."

I feel special that there are things about me someone could miss, and not just someone. *Alex.*

"I have to go take care of the dogs," I say. "And I have to start dinner at some point. Is that okay? Is this the most boring way to hang out? I realize I'm not cool."

"I'm having fun," he says. "And, Jules, you get that I'm not cool either, right?"

"You have residual manufactured cool," I say with a smile.

"I'll take that." He sits back in his seat and buckles his seat belt. "We need to walk the dogs, yeah?"

The dogs can clearly barely believe it that Alex is at the house; they circle him frantically, and after a quick sniff in my direction, they're back to basically assaulting him with affection. We leash them up and take off from the house down High Crest Avenue. I know it's pretty public, and therefore risky to be out in my own neighborhood with Alex, but I think danger is unlikely off the main streets.

"Did you get both of these guys at the shelter?" Alex asks me.

"Daisy we did, two years ago," I reply. "The shelter wasn't there when we got Peanut, which was when I was in fifth grade. We had another dog then, Rochester, who my moms got before I was born. But he was getting really old by then, and I think they knew we wouldn't have him for much longer."

"Oh, man," Alex says. "Now I'm really sad for fifth-grade Jules."

I smile at him. "She got through it. Clearly. Anyway, we were at this farmers' market to get fruits and veggies for the week, and a rescue group was there, and I fell in love with Peanut, and Mom and Darcy adopted him on the spot."

"Were people ever weird to you?" he asks. "Having two moms? Not that it's okay if they were, or that I assume it—"

"Alex, I know." I place my hand on his forearm for just a moment. "In general it hasn't been an issue. When I was little, I didn't know I should have to worry that people wouldn't be okay with it. I remember being in kindergarten and first grade, and when people said it was impossible I had two moms and no dad, I thought they were crazy. I mean, how could it be impossible? That was my life!"

A car passes us, and then stops. It doesn't park; it just pulls to a stop right there on La Loma Road. It's as this happens that I remember Thatcher and I discussing once how we don't live that far from one another. Of course we've never been to each other's houses, but I did have this knowledge.

I wonder if my brain conveniently let go of this knowledge earlier because it wanted this afternoon with Alex. It wanted a long walk in the afternoon sunshine.

Actually, that doesn't sound like my brain at all. I worry other parts of my body might be at play here.

"So, hey," Thatcher says, getting out of his old VW Golf. "What's up, guys?"

199

"Stray Rescue," I say quickly. "These dogs need homes."

"Jules, those are your dogs," he says. "They're wearing designer collars, and you have photos of them all over."

"I really like that Jules is a bad liar," Alex—the traitor—says. And then *he laughs.*

And *then* Thatcher *joins in.*

"Stop it, you...you boys," I say. "Thatcher, please don't tell anyone. I'd be the laughingstock of my entire staff."

"Whoa," Alex says. "That makes me feel great."

"I couldn't care less about...whatever *dog-walking* situation this is," Thatcher says. "I don't think anyone else would either."

"You know what I'm saying. You would too! No one would respect us anymore, Thatcher, and you know it. Maybe you would, because you're so terminally chill, but that's it."

"Okay, whatever," Thatcher says. "See you guys tomorrow."

"You're not going to tell anyone, right?" I ask. "Like Em? Especially Em—oh my god, no, telling Carlos would probably be worse. But Em could tell Sadie and—"

"I'm not going to tell *anyone*," Thatcher says. "But, seriously, no one would care."

He gets back into his car and drives off. I close my eyes and inhale deeply, hoping that my heart rate returns to normal.

"That was a...strong reaction," Alex says. I search his voice for his laugh, but it's not there.

"You're the enemy," I say. "I'm your enemy."

"You're just Jules," he says. "To me. That whole thing...

made me feel pretty shitty. My last girlfriend . . . she'd get super embarrassed whenever Chaos 4 All came up. It made me feel terrible about myself. And this? Just felt a lot like that."

"But you know we're secret! I literally just explained all of this! Why would we be secret if you thought things would be okay in public?"

We keep walking because of the dogs, but now it feels less like an afternoon in the sunshine and more like the first Stray Rescue shift after we broke up. It's dog walking in tandem by necessity.

"I'm doing that for you," he says. "I know you felt better that way. I don't love it, but it's what you wanted. Hearing all of that, though? Shit."

"I'm sorry," I say. "Please don't hate me. I just need to save the paper for next year. Okay?"

"I don't hate you," he says, but we don't hold hands on the way back to my house, and I'm worried if it's possible to lose something in such a short amount of time.

Again.

CHAPTER TWENTY-ONE

I sit down next to Thatcher in fourth period the next day and give him a look I trust says all that's needed to be said.

"Really," he says. "No one cares."

"'No one cares'?" I ask. "As in *people know*?"

"I forgot I have to be so careful with how I phrase anything to you," he says. "No one would care. I know, and I don't care. Others' feelings would reflect my own."

"Not necessarily," I say. "And I want you to know that this won't affect how I lead the team. The *Crest* is everything to me and—"

"'Everything'?" he asks.

"It's a priority," I say. "You know that. And we're already talking too much about this."

"Fine." Thatcher sighs. "Jules, what's your endgame?"

"We save the paper," I say. "The *Crest* doesn't shut down next year. You know that."

"So then you can...go public about all of this? This is going to stay a big secret until—"

Carlos sits down behind us. "What's the big secret?"

"Nothing," I say. "Thatcher's being overdramatic. You know how he gets."

Carlos cracks up. "Sure. You guys have something amazing planned against TALON or something?"

"Not yet," I say, as I've read you should never say you don't have an idea, even when you're blank.

"I...may have something," Thatcher says.

"Thatcher!"

"Jules, calm down," he says. "No, I've got something good on Natalie but...I have to implicate myself in it too. It's why I've held off."

"Did you go out with Natalie?" I ask, even though I can't imagine Natalie going out with anyone. To be fair, a couple of months ago I couldn't imagine it of myself either.

"*No*," he says. "I'll run home between meetings today and get it to show everyone. Carlos, you'll have to hack—"

"*Access* the system?" Carlos asks.

"Right," Thatcher says.

I bet Carlos would be really great at a secret relationship if he had to be. He could be having one now for all I know.

"Yes, I can access the system." Carlos nods in a manner I can only interpret as *with pride*. "Whenever I want."

"Question," Thatcher says. "Last year, was that your—"

"Do not answer that," I say. "Carlos, you're great, but I don't want to know about your butt."

♥ ♥ ♥

I stand outside Carlos's before our secret meeting starts. Everyone says hi and walks past me, until Tessa walks up.

"I can't let you in," I say. "Unfortunately there's no way to know that we can trust you again."

"I'm sorry," she says, and I can tell she's about to start crying again. I hate to see anyone cry, but I will not let it deter me. "I won't talk to Natalie again. Mr. Wheeler and I had a long talk and…"

"And?" I ask.

"And I'm sorry," she says again.

"I believe you," I say. "But I unfortunately still can't let you in. You've betrayed all of us, Tessa. You let your own team down."

"I won't have a ride home," she says in a wavering voice. "Amanda's my ride."

"That's not my problem," I say, and let myself into the house. Since I'm not a monster, I let Amanda know what's going on. Considering we have to wait for Thatcher to retrieve whatever he needs to from his house, I tell her she can take Tessa home now if she wants.

"All right," Thatcher says when he finally arrives, holding a DVD. "Carlos, can you fire this up?"

Thatcher makes a noise, somewhere between a sigh and a groan and a weird mumble. "I can't even ask all of you to respect me after this. So if you don't, I get it."

The video is of a dance recital. The little kids aren't really dancing, per se, just singing and performing choreographed movements. No one's particularly *good*, because they're probably four or five years old, but two kids stuck at the very end are particularly bad, and that's where the camera focuses most.

"Oh my god," I say aloud. "That boy is you."

"I wanted dance to be my calling," Thatcher says. "Alas."

"How can a kid be so bad?" Carlos asks. "Usually kids are at least cute. You look..."

"Angry," Marisa says. "You look angry. It's like dance is making you rageful."

"That girl next to you is worse," I point out, though picking on little kids feels mean, even during wartime. "That girl's terrible. Oh my god!"

"Yep," Thatcher says.

"Oh my god," I say again as it dawns on me.

And then Carlos and I say it together: "That girl's Natalie."

"Whoa," Marisa says. "I've never seen Natalie be bad at anything. Much less..."

"*So* bad," I say.

"We'll play it on Friday," Thatcher says.

"It doesn't have to be Friday," I say. "Right? Can't the system be accessed whenever we want?"

We decide to run the video on Thursday, to hopefully give people a full twenty-four hours to talk about Natalie's performance before TALON's next episode. If we were dealing with anyone else, I know that this wouldn't be a very big deal; most kids have done something silly in public that they'll wish they could take back later. But this is *Natalie*.

I didn't tell Darcy and Mom exactly how late my meeting would last, so when we head out for the night, I drive to Alex's instead of my house. He's waiting outside by the time I pull up, and any residual thoughts about the *Crest* evaporate when he sits down in my car.

Alex directs me to take a couple of turns and then to park on a semi-empty block. I give him what I hope is a cute and quizzical look, and he responds by climbing over the console into the backseat.

Oh my god. We are old-school *parking*.

I'm not sure I can gracefully hurtle the console, so I go the old-fashioned way by getting out of the car and then getting into the back. I never thought that the backseat of a Toyota Camry would be the most romantic setting I'd ever encountered, but it turns out that it's a very good place for kissing someone in the moonlight.

"The weekend after next," he says later, while I'm driving the few blocks back to his house, "my parents are going to some huge banquet for my dad's department."

"Cool," I say. "Is it all about mathematics or—"

"Jules." He cracks up. "The department rents a bunch of

suites at a hotel near the convention center. They'll be out most of the evening and all night."

"Next weekend?"

"The weekend after next." He kisses me again. "Two weekends from this one. I just thought you should know."

I know very quickly what he means, though even with a boy I kiss in cars, I hadn't thought that sex would be a thing I'd have to think about this year. It was something else I figured that I'd worry about in college or even grad school.

But now that it's been implied, I realize I'm not having a knee-jerk reaction against it. I'm not having any reaction against it.

"Okay," I say. I worry Alex thinks I'm just affirming that I understand which weekend he's referring to. "We can definitely have sex that night."

"I—" He laughs again. "Okay. We definitely can. Write it down in your organizer."

"Don't joke about my organizer. It keeps me very—"

Now he's kissing my neck and it's very hard to concentrate on speaking.

"Organized?" he says finally.

"You're mean," I say, and kiss him again. "You're the meanest."

"And you're the most organized."

♥ ♥ ♥

Sex, or at least the very real fact that it may soon be a very real part of my life, is unfortunately still on my mind when I get home. I'd hoped for some time off to help Mom with dinner, get through my homework, and talk to Sadie for long enough to make up for turning off my phone last night. But I'm in the midst of chopping veggies in the kitchen when it's all back, at full volume, in my head.

"Um," I say. "Can I go to the doctor?"

"Oh no," Mom says, dropping her meat tenderizer onto a pile of chicken. "Are you feeling sick?"

She washes her hands while I try to make the rest of my thoughts come out, but it's too late. She's already checking to see if I have a fever, as if mom hands work better than thermometers. When they're both home, it's even more annoying.

"Not that kind of doctor," I say.

"Like a therapist?" Mom asks. "Of course. This year's been so stressful for you, and with your worries about college...I know Joe's been concerned—"

"Alex and I are...sort of...I..."

"Having sex?" Mom asks.

"No," I say. "Not yet. But maybe. I don't know. It's like now it *exists*."

Mom nods. She doesn't look horrified or disappointed or, really, any different than usual.

"Obviously, of course, I knew it *existed*," I say. "But..."

"Of course, Jules," Mom says. "But I didn't even realize you and Alex were that serious—"

"This has been a strange week," I say. "Please don't tell anyone. I know you'll tell Darcy, but, no one else. Please?

We aren't officially…anything. With everything going on between TALON and the *Crest*, it's better if people don't…"

"Sadie doesn't know you're back together, is what you're saying."

"Well, Mr. Wheeler doesn't either, and he's my advisor for the *Crest*, and I know how you guys like to have weird conversations with him all the time."

Mom sighs loudly and goes back to pounding pieces of chicken for our chicken piccata. "Jules, I know it continues to be hard for you to believe, but Joe is our neighbor and friend, and we have what I believe to be *very normal friend and neighbor* conversations. I certainly don't tell him every time someone in the house goes to the gynecologist."

"*Every* time?"

"*Any* time," Mom says. "Do you want me to take over on the zucchini?"

"No, I can handle it. I'm fine." I start chopping again. "Wait, do you think I need therapy?"

Mom laughs. "Only if you want to go. But, honey…"

I stop chopping. She stops pounding. I wait for it, the sex lecture I should have seen coming.

"I think Darcy and I are both worried about what will happen if you don't get into Brown," she says.

"Well, me too!" I quickly see from her expression that it was the wrong answer. It's funny how I have none of her DNA but we're both terrible at hiding our emotions in such similar ways.

Darcy's better, because you can't be a successful attorney without a good poker face. "Hopefully I'll get in, and it won't matter."

"If you don't, do you promise me you'll talk to someone?"

I nod.

"Hey," Darcy says, walking in. "Oh, god. Why do you both look like someone's died? Who died? Did someone die?"

"Apparently just my sanity," I say, and it wasn't supposed to be a joke, but they both laugh, and that's probably for the best.

♥ ♥ ♥

When I go upstairs to my room later, I do open my organizer. I've already written in the box for two Saturdays from this one, the same thing I've written in every Saturday's space. *8 AM Walking dogs at Stray Rescue.*

I draw a heart in the remaining space.

CHAPTER TWENTY-TWO

I try not to visibly sit forward in anticipation on Thursday. It's not that I think we won't be the primary—or *only*—suspects for the video, but I still don't want to appear too knowledgeable or ready for it.

I never imagined myself breaking so many rules, much less during my senior year. I should probably be worried about my permanent record or disciplinary action, but the *Crest* and its legacy are far more important right now.

The TVs switch on, and I guess thanks to TALON, no one seems that surprised that it's happening, even on a non-TALON day. The footage has been edited down to start with a tight close-up on Natalie, and I'm worried no one will know it's her, but I hear her name being whispered around the classroom almost immediately.

"Everyone," Ms. Cannon says. "Please be quiet and watch the presentation."

Sometimes I can't tell if Ms. Cannon isn't that good at her job, or if she's just very, very over it.

"Where did you get this?" Sadie whispers to me.

"Thatcher," I whisper back.

"Oh my god!" Sadie shouts. "Thatcher!"

The transmission cuts out once the video ends, and Ms. Cannon sighs very loudly before directing us back to our discussion questions. The dance recital footage didn't get quite the reaction that the Chaos 4 All video did, but I have to believe that Natalie's fuming right now.

♥ ♥ ♥

"Hey." Natalie walks up to me at my locker after class. "Screw you guys. That was completely unprofessional."

"Oh, unlike stealing computer keys from all our keyboards? Or hacking into media files and substituting unapproved material into a publication?" I ask.

"The guest column should be open to everyone," Natalie says. "I'm a member of the Eagle Vista Academy student body."

"Then you should have followed protocol to submit a piece," I say.

"You're lucky I'm not going to take this to administration," she says.

"No luckier than you are that we're not doing the same."

"Your team should really proofread with more care," she says.

Alex walks by and comes to a halt upon sight of the two of us. He looks to me, then quickly away, and then back to Natalie.

"Come on, Alex," Natalie says. "Let's not waste our time with print media."

He sneaks me a little glance as they walk off. Alex is so *good* at secret looks that I feel my face heat up.

"Is it hard fighting your ex-boyfriend?" Amanda asks me as she and Carlos walk up to me.

"No," I say. Hopefully everyone will attribute my face—if it is as red as it feels—to ex-boyfriend anger and not current-secret-boyfriend-secret-looks feelings.

"Jules likes a competition," Carlos says. "Way more than she likes some boy bander."

"I—" I cut myself off from saying more, which is that of course I care more about the people in my life than I care about the *Crest*. I'm not sure what's true right now.

I have a text when I sit down in class, even though we've mainly been eschewing digital communication in this second round of our relationship. For your sake didn't want to risk dropping anything at your locker right now. But this might all be easier if we just came clean.

I start approximately one million messages to him, all with a variation of Are you crazy?? before landing on something much calmer. It's probably not the right time. Let's wait until the battle dies down.

Considering that there's no way I can see that happening before the *Crest*'s legacy is saved for the foreseeable future, I think I'm safe from worrying about coming clean for a while.

♥ ♥ ♥

Instead of going to school the next morning, I drive myself to a nearby medical complex. Answering real questions to a real medical professional ("No, I'm not sexually active. Yes, I plan to be.") is somehow my first real conversation about what's going on with Alex and my potential sex life. I thought I'd be embarrassed, but it just feels like a reminder that I'm not talking to anyone I expected to about this surprising development. I can't believe I'm not texting Sadie every detail. I can't believe I don't have her responses to get me through any of this. So I actually feel relief saying these things aloud, especially to a doctor, as she has no stakes in the rivalry between TALON and the *Crest*.

The actual exam is less awkward than I expect, though afterward, a nurse does teach me how to use a condom via a banana. I'm curious what happens to the bananas once they've served their demonstration purpose. It would be awful to just throw perfectly good bananas away when there are so many hungry people in this city. But it also doesn't seem right, somehow, to feed someone a banana that recently was wearing a condom. Now I'm worried I'll never be able to eat a banana again.

"Where were you?" Sadie asks when she finds me by my locker after third period. "You missed Jenni Gant asking a really stupid question about Mesopotamia, and Ms. Cannon nearly losing her shit."

"Doctor," I say, because in general my knee-jerk reaction is honesty.

"Are you sick?" Sadie asks. For just a moment I fear that she's about to check my forehead for a fever. Can I fake a fever? Can I direct heat to my head? "Why are you here if you're sick?"

"Just a checkup," I say, even though my purse feels weighted down suddenly with the condoms and birth control prescription we aren't talking about. I wonder if I should tell Alex about my appointment. Would Sadie?

"You promise me that you'd tell me if you were dying," Sadie says. "Right?"

"I promise I'm not dying, no more than regular mortality," I say. "Though after next year we'll be so far away it wouldn't really matter, right?"

Sadie narrows her eyes. "What's that supposed to mean?"

"Just, college?" I clarify. "Once you're off doing amazing things in New York, you won't have time to worry about my mortality anymore."

"I would never not have time for you, Jules," she says. "And I barely even see you now, and we live in the same zip code and go to the same school."

"It'll be different," I say. "You'll be having some new exciting adventure every day."

"So will you," Sadie says, even though I'm not sure how I'll think of anything to do outside of school and volunteer work without Sadie's help. "We'll still *talk*. We'll text, at least. If I can text you now, I can text you then."

"Okay," I say, even though I can't envision what that will actually be like. I didn't actually mean to get onto the subject of college at all, though I guess it's better than continuing to avoid conversation about my doctor visit. Talking to Sadie without talking about any of the things I actually want to talk about is yet another challenge I didn't expect to take on this year.

"How was TALON today?" I ask. I almost asked Mom to reschedule my doctor's appointment so I wouldn't have to miss it, but it'll be up on VidLook anyway.

"It was fine?" Sadie shrugs. "Alex toured a digital media company and made it almost seem interesting."

I know that Alex probably didn't think that it meant something against me to do a story like that, but I'm sure Natalie did. I'm sure it was Natalie's idea.

"How did Natalie look?" I ask.

"Not completely destroyed by the school's knowledge that she can't dance, if that's what you're asking." She closes her locker. "See you at lunch."

I want to call Sadie back and say the right thing—because lately it feels like I'm not doing that, and maybe even sometimes I'm saying the wrong thing. But if she doesn't fully understand about TALON, and she can't know about Alex, I don't know what that right thing would be.

On Saturday I stay late after walking dogs to help stuff envelopes for the annual Rescue Festival they're holding in a few weeks. Tricia buys us lunch, and when we're finished eating, since I haven't heard from Alex yet, I decide to walk dogs for a bit longer. It's not that without Alex I have nothing to do, but it's been *days* since we were curled up in the back of my car together.

I had no idea how long days could seem.

At home I sit down with my parents at the kitchen table while they're drinking wine (I'm given sparkling water) and snacking on fruit. I glance down at my phone while Mom and Darcy are discussing gardening or something backyard-related. Alex still hasn't texted, but Thatcher has.

Which is a first.

Feel free to shut her down. It won't be suspicious. And then: Or don't. Up to you.

I check my email. My parents are debating the pros and cons of rock gardens while I wait to find out who *her* is and what *suspicion* I'm avoiding and whether or not I should *shut her down*.

to: the-crest-staff@emailgroups.com
from: marisajohnston@email.com
subject: More Operation TALON

Hi everyone,

I know it's been a while since we discussed this. But I've been doing a lot of research, and I finally completed my article.

I did some investigating, and actually got in touch with someone else from the group, and there's definitely more to Alex Powell and Chaos 4 All than people know. I know that you're thinking, "No one cares that much about Chaos 4 All anymore, Marisa," but I think this ties into TALON's success on VidLook, believe if or not.

If we're looking to break into more long-form investigative journalism, this could be a good start. Plus I think this is a topic people actually will want to read about.

—Marisa

Oh no.

It has to be suspicious if I try to shut this down, though, despite Thatcher's text-based assurances. I'm figuratively and literally the leader of the Destroy TALON faction. Why would I suddenly want to stop a piece of long-form journalism that would not only guarantee readership but go after one of our main enemies? Yesterday Carlos publicly said that I cared way more about the competition than Alex's feelings.

Oh no, oh no.

On the other hand, of course, I want to know what it says. Earlier this week I might have kissed Alex in the moonlight, but right now I want to know what the *more to him* is. I think back to conversations we've had, how there were things he didn't even want to talk about, things that (possibly?) haunt him (is *haunt* too strong a word?) still.

Oh no, oh no, oh no.

alexpowellchaos4all.doc is attached. Download?

I click *yes*.

CHAPTER TWENTY-THREE

CHAOS 4 WHO?

HOW A FORMER BOY BAND MAY HAVE RIGGED THE SYSTEM AT E.V.A.

BY MARISA JOHNSTON

Two years ago, Chaos 4 All had the biggest hit of the country: on the radio, on iTunes, and online. "Want 2 B Ur Boy" set new records for viral popularity and sharing statistics. The music group enjoyed traditional success as well, including charting at #1 on Billboard's the Hot 100. Much of its publicity, though, including performances on all late-night shows and a *Rolling Stone* cover, stemmed from this never-before-seen rise to the top starting from the ground floor of the Internet.

Chaos 4 All's fast success, however, may not be what it seems, and the circumstances surrounding them may cast a popular club at E.V.A. in a different light.

Ethan Summers, a former member of Chaos 4 All, still lives in Chicago, where the group began over two years ago. "I saw a sign for auditions at Woodfield Mall," Summers told the *Crest*. "My friends made fun of it, but I secretly memorized the website address and went home and signed up. You just had to submit a head shot; I didn't have one, so I sent my freshman-year photo."

The members of Chaos 4 All didn't know each other before they were selected for the group by its manager, Len Whitley, who at the time Summers believed to be a stranger to all group members as well.

"I met Austin [Marts], Luis [Rivera], and Alex [Powell] during callbacks," Summers said. "We all went to different schools, but we hit it off pretty much right away. Our audition song was 'Want 2 B Ur Boy,' and we sort of naturally picked up on the harmonies when we sang together. I thought, if I get chosen for this gig, I hope these guys do too."

Summers's wish came true, as Marts, Rivera, Powell, and himself were selected by Whitley. When the four arrived at their first rehearsal, they met Chaos 4 All's fifth member, Johnnie Blakely. The other members did not recall seeing him at initial auditions or callbacks, but were quickly impressed by his singing and dancing abilities.

"Johnnie didn't hang out with us as much, outside of rehearsals," Summers said. "The four of us were pretty tight-knit, but it was like he had his own things going on. It might have bothered us more except that rehearsals took up so much time, we didn't have *that much* real free time as it was."

After a strenuous several weeks of rehearsals, Chaos 4 All recorded "Want 2 B Ur Boy" and filmed the music video. The rest of their self-titled debut album was recorded while the music video was being edited, despite that their *Rolling Stone* interview quotes Blakely that they'd worked on the songs together for months before they had any plans of making them public.

"We were just five friends goofing off," Blakely said in the cover story. "Or at least that's what it felt like. We never thought this would be anything more."

The "Want 2 B Ur Boy" music video broke 1.3 million views on VidLook on May 3 of that year. The video had supposedly been uploaded by Whitley only two days previously, on May 1.

"It was crazy to see how fast those numbers went up," said Chaos 4 All member Alex Powell. "I think we were all shocked."

According to Summers, though, these million views weren't what they seemed.

"Johnnie's dad was one of the original investors in VidLook," said Summers, and a review of VidLook's public investor information confirms that John Blakely II was one of VidLook's first and biggest investors. "He had power over the whole website. All he had to do was talk to the tech team, and they'd do whatever he asked."

According to Summers, that million-impression mark wasn't reached by a surge of viewers across the world tuning in to watch Chaos 4 All, but a simple and invisible tweak on the back end of VidLook's system. With the flip of a figurative switch, Chaos 4 All were an overnight success.

A search on blog postings over this short time period indicate that despite the staggering rise in views, there is no record of any sharing or embedding of the video over those few days. Normally a quick rise in popularity on VidLook is accompanied by a proliferation of bloggers sharing the content that then takes on a viral nature once social media gets its hands on it.

"Once we had those views, it didn't matter anymore where they came from," Summers said. "We were featured on the home page, and on the sidebar of almost every other video—music-related or not—on VidLook. And then people *were* watching, legitimately, and it took off from there. Moving forward, the rest of the fans were all real."

While those fans and the inevitable stardom that followed may have been real, they followed on the heels of something entirely unearned. This factor of unwarranted achievement came to prove itself out, when Chaos 4 All's next few singles saw less and less attention, until their fourth single, "Y Aren't We 2gether, Girl?," did not even crack the Hot 100.

"Once the last single off the album came out and tanked, I think we all knew that was it," said Powell. "There was a point in time where we thought we'd get to do this forever, but I guess there was always a part of me that thought we couldn't last."

Today the members of Chaos 4 All are, for the most part, living average lives away from show business. The only former member who appears to be actively pursuing a music career is Blakely. Blakely, who did not respond to attempts to interview him for this story, maintains a Bandcamp page featuring solo music available for a donation of six dollars.

Chaos 4 All is now frequently cited as an example of how fast viral success may not translate to long-term career success. Within E.V.A., there's another example of this: the weekly video and online program, TALON. While one might expect TALON's episodes to collect, at most, as many views are there are students at E.V.A., TALON episodes regularly list five, ten, and even beyond 20 times that number of views.

Now, with Chaos 4 All's VidLook tampering brought to light, a common thread, besides unrealistically high interaction numbers, is Alex Powell. Could Powell be using the lessons learned from Chaos 4 All to help this new extracurricular get off the ground?

CHAPTER TWENTY-FOUR

Relief is what I feel first. It's not *the worst*, even though up until this very moment I didn't realize that I even had a *worst* in mind. It was years ago, and it ended. It's nothing that changes our romantic relationship.

And what Chaos 4 All did probably isn't illegal.

But it's definitely unethical.

What Alex did was unethical.

And he's possibly still doing it.

After all, if Ethan Summers can be so casual about it now, they must have all known. Sure, they were all just fifteen, but couldn't someone have said something? Maybe they couldn't have stopped it, but they could have spoken up.

It really *should* make me upset. Doesn't this make Alex a thief, at least kind of? It makes him at least a liar. It makes him *a cheater*.

I'm actually not sure there are that many things worse than cheating.

I escape my parents and hole up in my room because I'm not sure how I'll manage not to tell them about this. They've literally been the only people I could talk to about Alex since we got back together, but now it's too much.

Peanut and Daisy join me on the bed, so I talk to them instead.

"We clearly can't publish it," I say. "It's all based on hypothesis at this point, and even if it wasn't, I'm not sure that Mr. Wheeler would let us."

I might be imagining it, but it seems like Daisy's giving me a look of concern.

"But of course it's not just that," I say while stroking Daisy's velvet ears. "I can't do that to Alex. Even if it's true. Even if he's a cheater and a liar and other bad things. He's still Alex."

Peanut perks up at the sound of Alex's name, which would be the cutest thing ever if not for the situation at hand.

"How could he know all of that?" I ask. "How could he *know that* and *go along with it*? Alex was so concerned when he did that Stray Rescue piece for TALON that I thought of him doing it for good and not for attention. Could someone like that cheat *everyone* just to get famous? And then *do it again*?"

My phone buzzes, and I look at it, even though I know who it'll be, both because I'm expecting it and because this is exactly how my life works. Of course it's Alex.

Want to go out? Obviously you have to drive. I'll buy dinner, or whatever else you want.

"Of course I want to go out!" I say, and I don't even pretend I'm talking to the dogs anymore. I'm just a girl, sitting on my bed, talking to myself. "But can I *not talk* about this? I don't think that's even possible."

Right now it seems that my phone is the source of everything stressful, so I stick it under my pillows and run back downstairs. Darcy and Mom are debating where they should go out for dinner, and even though I think it might be some kind of date night, I pipe up that French sounds great. I have to get out of the house. And I think when you're a parent, you accept that your child will at least occasionally hone in on your plans.

I hope so at least.

When we get back from dinner at Canelé and then coffee at Bon Vivant, Mom and I take the dogs out for a walk while Darcy checks in on some work emails. By the time we've brought the dogs back in the house, I say good night and head up to my room. I want more enforced time away from my phone, of course, but I've crashed enough of their date night.

Alex hasn't texted any more, but, *crap*, Sadie has. Why do I keep forgetting her?

Are you free? I have to stay home with Jon but we could order food.

OK I guess you're IGNORING ME like usual but please come over if you get this, so bored watching these kung fu movies.

I ordered Indian because I haven't heard from you, but I got tons of extra, so you can still come over if you want.

I start to type that I was out with my parents, but obviously I'd normally have my phone on me, and also I'd normally pick dinner with Sadie over dinner with my parents. Nothing will add up if I can't include anything about Alex or the Alex article.

I do text Alex back, though. Sorry, out with Mom and Darcy. It's probably too late now. Sorry!

His response is immediate. Don't be sorry. It's not THAT late, but I know you run on Sunday mornings.

I want to view him with nothing short of intelligent suspicion, but now he's texting me and being considerate. The thought of kissing him is enough to put the article out of my head.

For a moment, at least.

Thanks for understanding, I text. Have a good night!

Will he know something's up? Normally we don't say good night; we text back and forth until it's harder to come up with complete thoughts, and then it sort of trails off naturally. But if Alex suspects anything isn't usual about tonight, he doesn't say it, merely wishes me a good night too.

♥ ♥ ♥

Sadie and Em are at my locker when I get to school on Monday. Alex passes by me, and I use every ounce of effort not

232

to react in any way. All at once I want to demand he explain everything about Chaos 4 All and TALON, but also I want to kiss him. And instead I have to do nothing.

"Big Saturday-night plans?" Sadie asks me, and I remember the texts I missed while my phone was under my pillow and I was out on my parents' date.

"I'm sorry I didn't text back," I tell her.

"Let me guess?" Sadie rolls her eyes. "Your phone died?"

"No, I..." I'm not sure what I can say that will sound real and also that won't sound like a cop-out. "The *Crest* stuff."

"Of course," she says.

"We hung out on Friday night," I say, because all of us ended up at a movie again.

"With everyone else," she says. "Come on, Em. See you in class, Jules."

"But..." I lock eyes with her. "We have first period together."

"Yes, Jules, I'm capable of remembering my own schedule. See you there."

They walk off toward Em's first-period class, and I slide all my books from my backpack into my locker. And when I get to women's history, Sadie doesn't look at me at all.

CHAPTER TWENTY-FIVE

I go to school like it's a completely normal Tuesday, even though my SAT scores are due to get posted today. There were only a few other Eagle Vista students there with me that day; I try to gauge when I spot, for example, Natalie in the hall, if she looks nervous. But she looks like she always does; completely together and completely unfriendly.

"I bet they'll be fine," Sadie tells me before women's history. We seem to be talking again, but I did make a point of it last night not to let my phone out of my sight, and to text Sadie a couple of funny pictures of the dogs. "Not fine. *Perfect*. I've never seen you choke. I have so much more to worry about."

"NYU's acceptance rate is four times higher than Brown's," I tell her. "You're fine."

"Wait, do you have every college's acceptance rate memorized?" she asks.

"Just the ones relating to me," I say.

"Aw! You memorized it because I'm your best friend?

That's somehow the nicest thing anyone's done for me in a while."

"It wasn't even that nice," I say, which makes her laugh. Hopefully we're back on normal footing. Better footing, at least.

It is easier not confessing everything to Sadie when we aren't hanging out constantly, though.

"Let's skip class and check your scores," she says.

"Skip class?" I give her my best disapproving look, even though it's true that women's history, and *my future,* start at the exact same time today, eight AM.

"Someone will give us a pass," she says, pulling me down the hallway to Mr. Wheeler's classroom. We file in with his freshmen.

"Jules, Sadie," he says. "Are you two lost? Ha-ha!"

Sadie laughs like this is a very funny bit. "Mr. Wheeler, could we use one of the computers for just a moment, and get a pass for first period?"

He sighs but waves us over to the row of computers as the bell rings. Sadie sits down and types in my email address into the Web portal. "What's your password?"

I lean past Sadie to enter my password (PeanutDaisy777), and then follow the directions I've saved in my inbox to get to my scores.

"Should I close my eyes?" Sadie asks as I'm logging in. "Do you need, like, one private second?"

"Hey, ladies," Mr. Wheeler says. "Please keep it down over there, okay?"

"Sorry, Mr. Wheeler!" Sadie calls. Loudly.

"You don't have to close your eyes," I whisper as my results load.

"You're *a rock star*," Sadie says in nothing approaching a whisper.

"I don't think SAT scores are what rock stars are known for," I say, but I can't help smiling. My numbers are higher than ever. These are Brown-worthy scores.

"Sadie, come on." Mr. Wheeler looks over from his attempt to observe the classroom for attendance. "We're having a class here."

"Jules, we have to celebrate," Sadie says emphatically enough that Mr. Wheeler gives her another stern look.

"Later," I tell her. "We need to go to class."

"We should get our passes and leave this classroom," she says, loudly enough that Mr. Wheeler just walks to his desk and writes out our passes.

Out in the hallway I take out my phone to message Darcy and Mom in our ongoing group text. It's usually about who walked the dogs last or if whoever's making dinner needs something picked up from Gelson's. This is better.

"Swork for coffee?" Sadie asks.

"We have class," I say.

"We have passes that keep us out of first period," she says, "as long as we're back before the bell rings. You're a genius and deserve a latte. Well, more than a latte, but right now I will buy you a latte."

I don't know how to say no to Sadie when she's right in

front of me, so I walk as calmly as I can beside her and realize that if our passes are held in viewing range that no one really gives us a second look. We're off campus before I know it, and then we're only a couple of blocks from Swork.

We get small iced lattes, because we feel confident we can finish them in the couple of blocks before we're back at the school. I check my phone while we're still off campus and fast-sipping our lattes, and my parents have both responded. **We knew you could do it! SO PROUD!!!** plus an emoji heart from Mom. **Yes, this is a non-surprise, but the best kind,** from Darcy, and then one more emoji heart from Mom.

"I think my mom learned emoji from your mom," Sadie says, glancing over my shoulder. "I get whole messages without words now."

"We should get back to class," I say.

"I know, I know." She grabs my empty cup and tosses both of ours in the trash can immediately before school grounds. "We can celebrate for real later, okay? After you walk the dogs tomorrow? I'll plan something cool that you'll love."

"Maybe," I say. "I have to check my schedule."

Sadie sighs. "I know, I know, I'm just Sadie, I can't help you with the *Crest* or with Brown. I'd never be able to figure out how to take down the whole of digital media in one fell swoop."

"What? No, just, my moms, homework, everything." I shrug because *everything* partially does include the *Crest* and of course taking down at least the digital media within our school.

"Sure," Sadie says, but like the word is something she has

to get rid of from her mouth as quickly as possible. "See you at lunch."

I didn't think it was possible to get these scores and feel this bad.

♥ ♥ ♥

Maybe it's my scores, or the caffeine in the iced latte, or Sadie's *sure* playing over and over in my head, but I'd somehow almost forgotten about the Chaos 4 All article.

"We're definitely publishing it," Carlos says during our after-after-school meeting. "Right?"

"I . . . don't know," Thatcher says, looking right at me.

"I don't think that we should." I aim for a firm and convicted tone, but my pitch sounds off. High-pitched and off. "It doesn't seem to fit the historic goals of the *Crest*."

"I thought this year we were trying to protect those historic goals," Marisa says.

"We are—"

"That's *exactly* what this will do," she interrupts me. "Right?"

There are a lot of positive-sounding murmurs around Carlos's living room.

"I don't think *historic goals* ever covered ruining a student's reputation," Thatcher says in a voice that sounds convicted but not crazy. I have so much to learn from Thatcher. *"Right?"*

There are positive-sounding noises for this too, but maybe not as many.

"Even if I thought this was the right thing to do," I say, "which I don't, Mr. Wheeler would never let us print it."

"That is correct," Thatcher says. "Let's just drop it."

"This feels *important*," Marisa says. "What Chaos 4 All did was..."

"Really screwed up," Carlos says.

"It was *wrong*," Marisa adds. "And somehow no one's looked into this before..."

"Probably because Chaos 4 All ended up such an epic fail," Amanda says, and now almost the entire room sounds affirmative.

And I know this is true; if people had continued listening to and loving and supporting Chaos 4 All, there would have been much more attention on them. This would have come out earlier. And even if nothing else changed from there on out, when Alex started school here, I'd have already known he was a cheater and a liar. I can't imagine I would have fallen for him then.

Staying fallen, though, is another story.

"How did you even get Ethan Summers to talk to you?" I ask.

"Seriously," Carlos says. "And you got Alex to admit it too, which is pretty incredible."

"Alex didn't come out and admit anything," Marisa says. "I told him I was writing a piece about viral popularity and new media, and wondered if he'd give me a few quotes. But once I talked to Ethan, all the information came forward, and it all fit together."

"Again, how did you even talk to Ethan?" I ask. "Why did Ethan want to tell you everything?"

"Alex set it up; I guess they're still friends. And Ethan sounded *relieved*, to be honest," Marisa says. "Imagine carrying around that big secret for years. Plus probably no one asks him about Chaos 4 All anymore."

I think of the secret bottled up within Alex. He must feel the same.

"I think we owe it to everyone to at least give Mr. Wheeler the option," Marisa says. "It can't be pure coincidence that TALON gets so many views. Who the hell would care about TALON who doesn't go to this school?"

"We'll have to give away so much if we do," I say. "I'm afraid these meetings will come up. Or everything else we've tried to do against TALON."

"I'll say I did it on my own," Marisa says. "I know how to keep secrets, Jules."

"It's investigative journalism," Carlos says. "It's a really well-written article. I think Wheeler would be impressed with it."

"I'm not sure about how Mr. Wheeler would feel," I say, "but I agree. It's well written, and this is exactly what print journalism can do that something like TALON couldn't."

"Thank you," Marisa says.

"But considering Mr. Wheeler"—*and Alex*—"let's just sit on it for now," I say. "We can keep watching their online traffic and see if it stays suspicious. If it does, we'll have good reason to take our findings to Mr. Wheeler."

Everyone makes affirmative noises, so I move the conversation along to our next topic. And I tell myself that even if Alex wasn't my secret boyfriend—oh my god, "secret boyfriend" never stops sounding ridiculous—I'd still say we should give it some time.

♥ ♥ ♥

The doorbell rings once I'm home working on physics and letting equations take up my brain space instead of Chaos 4 All. It's a deliveryman with flowers—unbelievably, for me.

No one's ever sent me flowers before, but I still know that the first thing I should do is check the card. I suspect Darcy and Mom are behind them, but I also hope that they aren't, at least a little.

To Jules,
Great job. You're Awesome.
Love, Alex

I touch the word *love* with my thumb. Alex could have just signed his name. But he didn't.

I worry he's a liar and a cheater. I worry he doesn't have any sort of integrity, where things like success and popularity are concerned. But I also worry about the heavy burden he's carried around with him, and what such a weight might do to a person.

A person who might love me.

CHAPTER TWENTY-SIX

The next afternoon, during Topics in Economics, the overhead announcement system squawks to life. This happens so infrequently that everyone turns to stare at it.

"Will Julia McAllister-Morgan please report to Mr. Wheeler's classroom? Repeating, will Julia McAllister-Morgan please report to Mr. Wheeler's classroom?"

Ms. Schmidt writes out a hall pass for me, and I try to say good-bye to Alex with a glance before heading out of the classroom.

"Jules," Mr. Wheeler greets me as I walk into his classroom. This is his free period, so the room is empty of anyone other than him. "I've had something of an emergency come up, so I need to talk to you about the *Crest*."

"Is everything okay?" I ask. "Did TALON do something?" *Did you hear about the article?*

"My dad—" Mr. Wheeler stops himself, and I hear his

voice catch somewhere between his chest and his throat. "He died."

"Oh my god," I say. "I'm sorry. I'm so sorry, Mr. Wheeler."

He waves his arms at me. "It's fine. Well, no, it's not—anyway, the point is that I'm flying back home now. Normally of course I'd have someone else take over as interim faculty advisor, but I'm comfortable with you taking care of the *Crest* while I'm out. You've more than proven that you'll take it seriously enough. I'll be back Tuesday, and I don't know how available I'll be until then."

"I can take care of everything," I say. "Don't worry."

"You'll have to approve this week's issue and send the files to the printer," he says. "Carlos can tell you where the files are saved, and I'll email you the directions to upload them. Just make sure to enter your email address instead of mine to get the proofs on Saturday morning. There's a limited window to approve it, so make sure you're on top of your email."

"No problem," I say.

"I know we're still finalizing lots of this week's content," he says. "But you'll do fine. If you're not sure on anything, just trust your gut, Jules. Okay?"

"Okay," I say as he hands over the folder of current submissions.

"Monday you'll have to sign for the printed copies," he says. "You've seen me do it a thousand times, so that's no problem. And as for the pizza—"

"I can pay for the pizza!" I say. It feels like the very least you can do when someone's dad is dead is pay for pizza.

"Keep the receipts, and you'll get reimbursed when I'm back," he says. "Thanks for everything, Jules. It's a huge relief knowing you'll be managing everything."

"Thanks," I say. "I'm so, so sorry."

He pats my shoulder. I'm not sure how old Mr. Wheeler is—we've asked him, but he's not particularly forthcoming—but I know that he's younger than my moms. He's not even forty yet. Whatever age he is is way too young to not have one of his parents anymore.

"Thanks, Jules. You've given me one less thing to worry about, and your mom—Lisa, that is—is going to run me to the airport."

"Good," I say, because even though I've never liked how friendly Mom and Darcy are with Mr. Wheeler, right now it makes sense. If you're far from home and your family, some-one has to step in when things happen. I suddenly feel so young to have never seen that before. "See you next week."

"See you then, Jules. Thanks again."

I walk back to Topics in Economics, and now that I'm not looking at Mr. Wheeler, something overtakes my sadness and sympathy. Mr. Wheeler asked me to take care of the *Crest*. He didn't call in another teacher or an administrator. He called in Jules McAllister-Morgan.

I'm in charge.

♥ ♥ ♥

By the next day, news of Mr. Wheeler's temporary departure has made its way around the school. It's not exactly the biggest gossip, but no one's surprised not to see him in our fourth-period class for the *Crest*.

"What sub are we stuck with?" Carlos asks. "Does anyone know?"

Everyone starts volunteering what they've heard about Mr. Wheeler's other classes, while I walk to the front of the room. A man's father is dead, so I try not to beam.

"I'll actually be handling this class for the next couple of days," I say. "So it'll just be business as usual."

"This is awesome," Marisa says, and I wait to be congratulated. "We can run the Chaos 4 All piece. Since Mr. Wheeler was the problem."

"That's your only concern?" I ask.

"Jules, I worked my ass off on that article," she says. "And you're the one so obsessed with preserving our print heritage or whatever."

"I'm not obsessed," I say, which might be a mistake because lots of people confuse passion with obsession, and that's probably why other kids flat-out *laugh* when I say it. "I care about preserving it, absolutely. I think it's my—our responsibility."

"I care about that too," Marisa says. "Think of how many people would be reading it if we were picked up by a major publication."

She's right. Natalie might have created TALON, but how important will that look next to coverage from national media?

"Okay," I say, but then I worry I'm making the decision too quickly. I have Mr. Wheeler to think about, and of course Alex. I'll be helping him let go of the guilt he must be carrying, but I wasn't prepared to be doing that this week. "Let's seriously think about moving forward with it."

♥ ♥ ♥

Alex wants to take me out to celebrate my scores, and even though I've been putting off time alone with him since I read the article, and even though I couldn't find time for Sadie, I agree to it that night.

"Hey." Alex grins at me once he's in my car and in between kisses. "Where do you want to go?"

"Anywhere," I say. "Well, not anywhere. But anywhere you want where people from school wouldn't be."

"Feels like a lot of potential places." He leans in to kiss me again. "What's, like, your favorite place here?"

"You've probably seen it," I say. "School or Stray Rescue maybe? *Oh!*"

"Jules McAllister-Morgan has an idea," he says.

"Have you see the ocean?" I ask. "Since you moved here?"

"I haven't," he says. "Let's go."

I pull the car into drive and head toward the 110 Freeway.

I'm not sure I've ever gotten on the freeway to drive so far this late. Everything seems open ahead of me right now, though.

"Can I ask you something?" I sneak a look at Alex, though of course I believe in responsible driving. "Why haven't you learned to drive yet? I'm not judging you, of course, I'm just curious."

"Of course you're not judging me." He laughs and trails his fingertips down my arm. "Look, I've tried. My mom tried to teach me, and when that didn't work, my dad tried to teach me. My friend Jack at my old school tried, and so did my ex-girlfriend—well, she wasn't my ex at the time."

I can't lie; I definitely had fantasies where I was the first person who actually made Alex learn how to drive. But if his Michigan girlfriend couldn't teach him, I'm not sure what would give me an advantage.

"I don't like feeling out of control," he says with a shrug. "Why put myself in a situation where I do if I can help it?"

"But you're *in* control," I say, my hands gripped on the steering wheel. "That's the whole point."

"It doesn't feel like it," he says.

We drive past downtown LA, its brightly lit skyline always a tiny surprise when it appears. Los Angeles doesn't feel like that kind of city, because the beauty it's known for is full of palm trees and ocean waves. But its urban beauty is striking too.

"It's strange that we'll be gone in a year," I say. "Maybe it's not to you, since you've moved before, but I've been here since I was born."

"It's weird I get to pick where," he says. "When your dad's a professor, you move for the schools, not the places themselves. It's not like I decided to move to Lawrence or Ithaca or Ann Arbor."

"Or here," I say.

"Or here. But here sounded good," he says. "In all the other places, it was... *really weird* to be the guy from Chaos 4 All."

A chill slips around and inside me, for just a moment.

"In LA, though... it's definitely not the weirdest thing."

"It's not weird at all," I say.

"Jules, it is," he says, laughing. "I won't think you're a jerk for admitting that."

I sneak a smile over at him before locking my eyes back on the freeway as I merge onto the 10. "I like that you're weird."

"Good!" He's still laughing. "Anyway, our part of LA isn't really... LA? We don't have a beach and we don't have Hollywood. It's just a normal town. Where people don't think Chaos 4 All is that weird. And where I can forget everything that happened."

Everything?

"I just want the next part of my life to be my choice," he says.

"You want to be in control," I say with a smile.

"I know that for someone like you that's never an issue," he says. "But me... I'm still working on it."

Traffic moves quickly until we get to Santa Monica, where the exit ramps clog with cars trying to get to restaurants, shopping centers, bars, and the beach. When we get out of the car once I've parked a couple of blocks from the sand, the cool ocean breeze wraps itself around us. We're only about thirty miles from our houses, but it's another atmosphere.

"Thanks for taking me here," Alex says as we arrive at the sand and pause to take off our shoes. "Do you want to walk in?"

"It'll be cold," I say. "And wet."

He cracks up, so loudly that people look in our direction. "Really, Jules? The ocean's going to be *wet*?"

"I just meant that we didn't bring towels or anything."

He kisses me softly. "I'll take my chances."

CHAPTER TWENTY-SEVEN

I'm exhausted when I sit down in women's history the next morning. I force all my energy into a smile at Sadie so that I won't have to make up a reason I'm so tired.

"Your favorite show's coming on," she says as the TV starts up for TALON.

Natalie starts off in her typical perfect newscaster way, and if there's any part of her that's still embarrassed to be known as an exceptionally bad dancer, even among children, it doesn't show on her face.

Natalie throws it to Kevin for the AroundTown segment, which apparently this week is just about places nearby where E.V.A. students hang out. There's footage of TALON staffers Jesse and Joramae hanging out in front of the fancy fountain at the Americana, and then a serious shot of Natalie at the downtown library. How can they take themselves seriously as journalists? It's literally just footage of students in places.

And then it's me. It's me, and it's Alex. It's me, and it's

Alex, and we're in front of Donut Friend, and we're holding hands. While I'm figuring out ways to explain that this must be old footage from the brief original time we went out, the street decorations for a local autumn celebration give us away.

I expect the room to react, but most people are just silently watching the next clip, which is of the camera crew in front of the big streetlamp art piece at LACMA. Most people, except for Sadie.

"Oh, *this* explains *everything*," she says.

"Miss Sheraton-Hayes," Ms. Cannon says. "No talking."

"I have to go to the bathroom," she says, loudly, while on-screen, kids are frolicking at the Grove. "Please."

I realize that Sadie's voice is breaking. Sadie must be *this close* to crying.

"Fine, Miss Sheraton-Hayes," Ms. Cannon says, writing out a pass. "Hurry back."

"Me too," I say, following Sadie up to the front of the room. "Please."

Ms. Cannon narrows her eyes but writes out another pass. "Be back by the time class resumes, girls."

I wait for the classroom door to shut behind us. "Sadie, I—"

"No," Sadie says as tears stream down her cheeks. When you've been friends with someone since infancy, you've seen them cry many times.

I had just never caused it before.

"You lied to me," she says. "You lied to *everyone*."

"I'm sorry," I say. "But with everything going on between the *Crest* and TALON—"

"No one cares about that," she says. "No one cares except you and Natalie, but instead of realizing it, or just trying to *be my friend*, you're letting your stupid newspaper—"

"The *Crest* isn't stupid," I say. "The *Crest* is the most important part of my senior year, maybe of all of high school."

Oh my god, why am I defending the *Crest* right now?

"Yeah, I've noticed," she says. "We've all noticed. You care about it more than you care about any of us. You know, Thatcher's on the *Crest* too, and I know he's involved in all your little plots, but he still manages to be a good boyfriend and be honest to Em."

"I'm not your boyfriend," I say.

"No, you're *my best friend*," she says. "Which should be equally important, if not more so. And you freaking *know that*, Jules. And Alex—"

"I wanted to tell you," I say.

"Then you should have. You've made me feel..." Sadie cries silently for a moment, and shoves my hand away when I try to touch her shoulder. "Like *nothing*. I know I'm just stupid Sadie with my stupid hair and my stupid problems and I'm not going to an Ivy League school, but—"

"You're not stupid," I say, and I try to touch her shoulder again. I can't hear Sadie talk this way about herself. "I just have so many important things going on right now."

"Yeah," she says. "I can see where I rank with all of that."

She turns from me and keeps walking down the hallway.

"Sadie, please let me—"

"Go back to class, Jules. Don't jeopardize your GPA."

She keeps walking, and I don't know what to do besides turning around and walking back into women's history. TALON's over, which means I missed Alex's piece, but did Alex know about the segment? Did Alex just want to come clean? Is Alex burdened with too much? He was a cheater in Chaos 4 All, and he might be a cheater for TALON, and then I made him take on this secret relationship.

He finds me in the hallway after class, and even though I feel like I should be looking for Sadie, who never came back to class, it feels really good to hug him without worrying about anyone seeing us. Now everyone can see us.

"I didn't know they were going to do that," he says. "I promise."

"I believe you," I say. "It's just Natalie being Natalie."

"Well…" He grins. "You guys did run that dance recital video. She owed you."

"Don't defend Natalie," I say, even though I guess they're friends or, at the very least, colleagues.

"Okay," Alex whispers right before he kisses me. I should be looking for Sadie, but I'm so relieved this right now is still safe and good, even with the whole world knowing. "It's good to have it out there, right? We needed the push."

"Yes," I say, and now I know that we're running the article. I can't wait for fourth period; I'll text Marisa as soon as I can.

Getting rid of secrets feels right; I'd imagine long-held secrets would feel even better to let go of.

"I should go to class," I say. "And try to find Sadie."

"She just walked by," Alex says, and that means that Sadie saw me with Alex's hand on my waist while I should have been looking for her. But I head off in the direction Alex points anyway, and I spot her blue hair easily in the crowded hallway.

"Sadie, can we talk?" I ask.

"I have to get to class," she says. "So, no."

"I'm sorry I didn't tell you. I *wanted* to."

She just keeps walking away, and I know I have to get to class, and I need to text Marisa, and so I let her go. In second period, Em treats me no differently than usual, and after sneaking a text to Marisa, I send one off to Sadie: I didn't mean to hurt your feelings. And then another: I'm free after my Crest meeting this afternoon. Can we hang out? And I can't help sending a third: Sadie, you're never nothing to me.

♥ ♥ ♥

"Are you serious?" Marisa greets me as I walk into fourth period. "We can run it?"

"*Yes*," I say, with Natalie's defeated face in my head—I mean, Alex's relieved face. Of course. I'm doing this for him. Yes, there's the bonus of hopefully ending TALON once and for all. If they're cheating their numbers, I can't imagine school administration would be happy with that.

Even if they aren't, there's no way that TALON can compete with the attention the article will get.

"We're running it?" Thatcher asks as Carlos runs around us to take a seat at one of the layout computers to switch out the "Fall into Extracurriculars!" headline for "Chaos 4 Who?" "You're okay with this, Jules?"

"Yeah, I didn't know you guys were back together," Carlos says, tweaking the headline's placement.

"I should explain," I say as the rest of the class surrounds us to watch Carlos work. "I never wanted any of you to think that I wasn't one hundred percent committed to the *Crest* and working against TALON. So I didn't want you to know about Alex because it might give the wrong impression about my loyalties."

"Alex is hot," Marisa says. "I think that's all I assume about your loyalties."

A few people agree with her, and then it seems like all anyone cares about is watching Carlos format the article.

"What happened to you not being sure if it's appropriate for the *Crest*?" Thatcher asks me.

"This is where print journalism excels," I say. "We still need to build readership, and national media attention would be a great way. And, of course, sometimes it's better for secrets not to be secrets anymore."

Thatcher doesn't say anything.

"Do you think it's wrong?" I ask.

"I'm not sure what I think," he says. "But you're in charge, so if you want to run it, let's go. I trust you, Jules."

It would be easy to stay in Mr. Wheeler's classroom during lunch to avoid whatever awaits me in the cafeteria, but it's another chance to talk to Sadie, so I go. Alex is already at the table with his lunch when I arrive, and everyone laughs or raises eyebrows or smiles knowingly at us. It should feel great, but *everyone* doesn't actually include Sadie, who's reading her women's history textbook and not looking at anyone with her red-rimmed eyes.

♥ ♥ ♥

After school we each proof a copy of this week's issue, and, miraculously, there are no typos or printing errors. Seeing it in print makes me feel even better about my decision today.

Besides the cover story, it's an incredibly typical issue of the *Crest*, but we did almost all of this one on our own. I'm sure Mr. Wheeler will mainly be thinking about his family when he gets back next week, but I also hope that he's proud of us. Normally, the *Crest* wouldn't even exist without the work our advisor handles, but Mr. Wheeler didn't even bother trying to have another teacher cover those duties. Anything that I didn't handle personally, I oversaw.

This isn't even a typical issue. I'm positive this'll be the most buzz-worthy issue we put out this year, and that's because of me. I did this all on my own—well, I did this with my staff. TALON might have caught us off guard initially, but I'll be the one who conquered.

And of course I care about journalism, tradition, and truth, but triumph feels really great too.

♥ ♥ ♥

Alex joins me for my shift at Stray Rescue on Saturday, and even though it's unprofessional, I let him cover for me a few times during walks so that I can check my email for the printer's proofs. Everything's perfect, and that means the issue is completed.

"Everything okay?" Alex asks, handing Giselle's leash back to me while he keeps Titus.

"Everything's great," I say. "Our extra proofing paid off, and our issue's perfect to go, and—is it strange that I'm talking about the *Crest*? I know that even though everyone knows about us that we're still at war."

"It's fine," he says.

"Make sure you read the issue on Monday," I say.

"I always read it," he says. "Well, I have been. Since we've been back together, at least. And in private."

"The article Marisa interviewed you for is in it," I say. "So read it in public."

He grins and leans over to kiss me.

I swat him away, but only after the kiss is over. "We're working!"

"You're very rule-abiding," Alex says. "Anyway, congrats. Sounds like Mr. Wheeler doesn't even need to come back."

"That would be amazing," I say. "He should stay where he is! Oh my god, except for that his dad's dead. I didn't mean—"

"Too late, Jules, now I know you're a terrible person."

I smile at him and he grins back. "Do you know what a week from today is?"

He looks confused, and after a moment or so, I realize he's messing with me.

"My parents are going to a banquet," he says. "And you're coming over."

"I'm on birth control," I say softly, and then switch back to my normal voice because I don't think that dogs understand what we're talking about. "Just to let you know. But I think we should use condoms too."

"I figured that we would," Alex says. "I'm not some irresponsible jerk, you know. I think I'm pretty nice."

"I know you are," I say, because no matter what he had to do with Chaos 4 All's success or TALON's numbers, I believe that.

CHAPTER TWENTY-EIGHT

On Monday I get to leave third period early so that I can sign for the papers. Carlos is allowed to join me, so we each cut open a box.

"This looks awesome," he says.

"It looks *perfect*," I say, and we high-five. In my head I picture Alex reading it and feeling free from his past missteps.

And then I picture Natalie. I picture Natalie for *much longer*. I think about the TVs never turning on again during Friday first periods, and the student body reading the *Crest* because it's the only place to get news about the school, and it'll be like Eagle Vista Academy—and my senior year—are back to where they were supposed to be.

And Sadie will understand now, because TALON's bad behavior is in print for everyone to see. She'll understand how seriously I had to take the battle. Sadie and I will be fine.

The pizzas show up after fourth period as the bell rings for lunch. The majority of the staff helps themselves as the freshmen sadly trudge out to hand out papers. My phone's out where I can see the screen, because I'm sure Alex will text.

And he does.

J. What the fuck.

"I have to go," I say, stumbling out of the desk chair. Suddenly it doesn't seem so obvious that the article would thrill everyone but Natalie.

The hallway looks like one of my fantasies. Everyone—*everyone* is reading the *Crest*. I've never, ever seen my school look so engaged in my paper. My lunch table is sitting quietly, reading the *Crest*. It's probably the wrong moment to realize I've never even seen my best friends look so engrossed in the paper.

"Guys, I have to—"

Sadie silences me with a look. "I guess the *Crest* won, huh?"

"No, I—guys." I make eye contact with Alex. Well, I try, but he won't look up. "Alex."

"This was the article I was interviewed for?" he asks. "And you didn't tell me?"

"Can we talk?" I ask. "Please?"

"Alex is really upset," Sadie says. "You being here is just making it worse."

"Why? I was trying to…I thought…" I start to cry. It's right then that I realize everyone near us is staring. People across the cafeteria are staring too. Basically the entire school is watching this happen. People are watching Alex looking more deflated than I've ever seen him, and it's not at all his fault.

To be completely fair, once upon a time, it *was* his fault. He lied and cheated in a huge way, but in the midst of falling in love with him, it was so easy to write that all off as Former Alex. Young Alex. The Past's Alex. On-screen Alex.

Not my Alex.

And now it seems like he's none of those Alexes anymore.

"Fine," he says.

We walk out into the hallway together, though we have to stick near the cafeteria entrance so we don't get into trouble.

"You were so relieved when TALON ran the video of us," I say.

Alex crosses his arms across his chest. "Uh-huh."

"And you'd mentioned...that there were things about Chaos 4 All you couldn't even talk about now," I say. "Your quotes to Marisa made it seem that way too. I thought you'd be so happy to just have it out there and not have to hide it anymore."

I hope it's okay to leave out the part where I wanted to beat Natalie.

"Jules, shit," he says. "I just meant that I hardly ever saw my parents and I felt like I didn't have control over my life and there's no way to really get ready for being that famous. Not that I cheated."

"I was trying to help," I say.

"I knew you cared about the rivalry more than almost anything, but I guess I was stupid enough to think I wasn't part of the *almost*."

"You weren't—you aren't. Alex, please. I only ran it for you." I hate how that's only partially true. Right? Oh, god, I don't like doubting myself. "I know you're mad, but—"

"I can't believe you'd expect me to believe that," he says. "If you ran it for me, why not check with me? Why link me to the TALON shit, when that's *recent*? There's no way you did this for me."

"You seemed relieved when we were finally public," I say, "as a couple. I thought this would be the same. And you were in the article!"

"You thought accusing me of faking my past success, and using that to fake TALON's success would...relieve me?" He shakes his head. "You were the first girl after all of that who I thought I could trust. I could be myself around you. Guess I called that wrong."

He turns from me and walks back into the cafeteria.

I numbly find myself walking back through the hallway and into Mr. Wheeler's classroom. Everyone's eating pizza and chatting, but they look up at me when I enter the room. I touch my face and remember that I'm crying.

"Jules," Carlos says.

"I don't want to talk to anyone," I say as I sit down at Mr. Wheeler's desk. No one moves or says anything for what feels like forever, but of course eventually everyone goes back to eating pizza and talking.

"Hey." Thatcher walks over to me. "You okay?"

"Obviously I'm not."

"I'm not really good at giving advice," he says with a shrug. "Maybe I should have talked you out of it."

"You couldn't have," I say. "I think I tricked myself into believing something so I could..."

I don't want to finish the sentence with *win*, and I'm glad Thatcher doesn't do it for me.

"Just be honest," Thatcher says. "There's the advice I'll give now. Be honest with everyone, especially with yourself."

When the bell rings, I drag myself to Topics in Economics. I've beaten Alex there, and I hurriedly scribble onto a piece of loose-leaf paper before he arrives.

> Alex,
> Please believe me. I'd never try to hurt you. I screwed up, but of course I care about you more than The Crest. I love you.
> -Jules

When Alex walks by I hold up the sheet of paper, but he just reaches down and balls it up into his fist.

None of my friends speak to me for the rest of the day,

though there's no such luck with the rest of the school. Even though my name's clearly not in the byline, people have questions about Ethan Summers, the research, and VidLook. I'm convinced I must look like far too much of a mess to be taken seriously, but when I duck into the bathroom to examine myself in the mirror, I look the same as always.

How does heartbreak look so normal on me?

♥ ♥ ♥

Natalie is waiting for me at my locker when the school day finally ends.

"Hi," I say.

She holds up a copy of the *Crest*. "We should sue you for libel."

"It all looks very suspicious," I say. "You can't deny that."

"Do you honestly think we'd fake our numbers?" she asks. "Do you think we'd *need* to?"

"Who outside of the school would even *care* about TALON?" I ask.

"Parents," she says. "Friends from other schools. We've reached out to journalists and other school video programs. It adds up quickly, Julia."

"Okay," I say.

"We'll put together something for this Friday," she says. "But I'll still expect a retraction in next week's issue of the *Crest*."

"I'll have to consult with Mr. Wheeler about that," I say, though that just reminds me that Mr. Wheeler doesn't know what we published, and tomorrow he will. How were my instincts so incredibly wrong?

"Do." Natalie drops the issue of the *Crest* at my feet and walks off.

At home I fly through my homework, and fake the best mood that isn't suspicious on a Monday for Mom and Darcy. There's so little I've kept from them, but the day has been rough enough. Hopefully it's fair to hold off on letting them know just how much their only, very expensive, daughter screwed up for another day or two.

My phone is silent, even though I keep praying that it'll beep with a message from Sadie or Alex or even Em or Thatcher with something comforting. When I check my email, it's a flood of messages, but it's hardly good news. Some sleazier celebrity blogs have picked up the story, and now the details aren't just ours. The story belongs to the whole world now, or at least the whole World Wide Web.

I wanted national attention, sure. But I didn't want that.

♥ ♥ ♥

Sadie doesn't look at me when I arrive in women's history the next morning, but at this point it doesn't surprise me. What does, however, is that moments after the bell rings, the overhead system squawks my name again, just like last week. Once it tells me to report to Mr. Wheeler's room, though, it doesn't seem like much of a mystery.

Oh my god.

I slowly gather my books and my legs are shaking as I walk down the hallway. I expect to see a class full of freshmen when I walk in, but it's empty besides him.

"I sent them to the library," he says at my confused expression.

"Oh," I say. And then, "Welcome back."

"I'm sure you know why I called you in here," he says.

"Yes," I say.

"Sit down, Jules." Mr. Wheeler sighs and picks up yesterday's issue of the *Crest*. "I don't even know where to start with this."

"Mr. Wheeler, I can explain everything, really."

"You're the one who's been talking about *legacy* all year, Jules," he says. "And I'm gone for less than *one week*, and you've brought the paper down to the level of a tabloid."

"Mr. Wheeler," I say, and this is the moment where I can't stop myself from crying in front of him. Mr. Wheeler has seen me in my pajamas, seen me fighting with my parents, and—though I've mainly blocked it out of my memory—once heard me singing a jingle for mayonnaise. But I'd relive any of those moments over crying.

"I know that you're right," I say finally. "I'm responsible for destroying our legacy."

He taps at a few keys on his computer. The printer comes

to life and spits out one single sheet of paper. From where I'm sitting it looks like a letter.

"I sent this off last week." Mr. Wheeler grabs the paper off the printer and hands it to me. "But I thought you should take a look at it."

"Mr. Wheeler, I—"

"You're dismissed," he says. "I'll see you later in class."

CHAPTER TWENTY-NINE

Dear Admissions Staff of Brown University:

I've known Julia McAllister-Morgan since the summer before her freshman year at Eagle Vista Academy. I coincidentally moved to a house next door to her family's, and through meeting her parents, met Julia as well. From the start she impressed me as a teenager mature beyond her years, with focus and dedication to school, despite the fact that her intelligence guaranteed she wouldn't have to try very hard if she didn't want to.

Julia joined the staff of the school newspaper, the *Crest*, at the beginning of her freshman year. It was apparent early on that her goal was to eventually earn the position of editor in chief. Due to her hard work and high standards over the next three years, I was pleased to offer this position to her at the start of her senior year. Often once students achieve the title of editor in chief, I notice that their work ethic slides a bit with this goal achieved and senior-year responsibilities/activities encroaching on time and attention. With Julia, this couldn't be further from the truth.

This year, a new weekly news show commenced at Eagle Vista Academy. Their school TV program and Internet presence has certainly taken away some of the *Crest*'s readership, as new media is liable to do to older forms. Julia was immediately concerned about protecting the legacy of the paper, even after being assured that the *Crest* was funded through her senior year. Her efforts to regain—and grow—readership had nothing to do with her personally, but the school's, and print media's, tradition.

This may give the impression that Julia is myopically focused on the *Crest*, but I'm aware she also handles duties for the Associated Student Body. In the hallways and during lunch, I've never seen her not surrounded by a large group of friends. And despite my declarations that I'm not at the stage of my life where I feel responsible enough for a pet, Julia's devotion to her volunteer work at a dog rescue shelter means that I've received many brochures about adoptable dogs in my area. This is all to say that while a devoted student, journalist, and leader, Julia is also a young adult with a full and diverse life.

Therefore, it's with the highest degree of confidence that I recommend Julia for undergraduate admission to Brown University. Her unstoppable spirit and clear desire to better the world will, no doubt, benefit your campus. She has definitely accomplished this at Eagle Vista Academy, and I'm excited to know she'll bring that energy with her next year to college.

Sincerely,

Joseph Wheeler
Academic Advisor, *The Crest*,
Eagle Vista Academy

CHAPTER THIRTY

I hope that by fourth period, we can just get back to normal, but Mr. Wheeler's anger is so palpable that even the freshmen know to slink in silently.

"I've already spoken to Jules," Mr. Wheeler says, "but I'd like to say that I'm disappointed in all of you. I'm sure many of you had absolutely nothing to do with this article, but I'm also sure that many of you did. There's no one in this room who should think that this is the type of story we should feel proud of publishing."

"It's gotten national media attention," Marisa says. "Isn't that good?"

Mr. Wheeler sighs. "For you, Marisa, I guess that it is. You've got something to put on your college applications next year. But for a school paper founded with intramural information and communication as goals, national media attention shouldn't have really been what we were aiming for. Marisa, you won't be writing any articles for two weeks. Jules will also be suspended from her duties for that time, as will Carlos, as that layout work is clearly his."

Mr. Wheeler shakes his head. "I wish I could discipline all of you, but obviously I can't write and design this entire thing on my own for two weeks, so that'll have to be it."

The class moves on to normal topics, but it's Mr. Wheeler collecting information, not me, and it's Amanda working in the layout program, not Carlos. Marisa keeps raising her hand with story ideas and then very quickly putting it down. The three of us aren't built to do nothing, and yet that's all we'll have for two weeks.

♥ ♥ ♥

I don't even attempt to walk to the cafeteria for lunch, but Em and Thatcher spot me on my way to the library and strong-arm me into walking with them. No one looks as severe as they did yesterday, though no one includes me in conversation either. All I want to do is write note upon note for Alex, *I love you*s and *I'm sorry*s and *I still want this weekend*s, but I can't stand the thought of my words crumpled up again in his hands.

Em leans over and scribbles into my notebook. *Don't worry, Jules—it'll all blow over*, she writes, amid doodled curlicues of wind. I try glancing up at Sadie. She doesn't smile, but she doesn't look angry either. I decide to take it as a positive sign, because it's all I really have. But after school, no one texts or emails me, and lunch is exactly the same the next day, and the day after that. Maybe Em is right about the anger blowing over, but I worry everything else is here to stay.

♥ ♥ ♥

On Friday, Natalie is seriously addressing the camera when TALON starts. I admit I'm jealous of her navy pin-striped blazer and the way her hair manages to be sleek and yet full of volume. I guess I might be jealous of less shallow aspects of Natalie too, like that she created this from nothing, and that people chose to follow her.

"Hello, TALON viewers. This week at Eagle Vista Academy, there were serious accusations made by the *Crest* against the validity of TALON's success on VidLook, and possibly beyond. I'd like to address these accusations on behalf of the entire TALON staff."

Natalie's voice-over runs over screenshots of the comment sections of their VidLook page, as well as responses from journalists on Twitter to promise to check out TALON. There's no direct proof that TALON didn't doctor their numbers, but it seems extremely unlikely.

They're exactly as successful as they claim to be. Natalie built herself something that works, and works well at that. I'm clinging to a crumbling empire past its glory days.

When Alex's segment begins, I'm relieved that he looks like himself and not like the shell of his usual self who's been in classes and across the lunch table from me this week. He's genuinely so good on camera. It's not just that he's cute (though of course he is) but he looks so comfortable, as if he was built just for this. In person, he's just a boy—an attractive and funny boy—but he'd probably blend into the crowd if not for Chaos 4 All. On-screen, though, he has all the confidence and charisma in the world. I realize my opinion could be biased, but I also see how other students lean forward in their chairs, watching Alex closely.

Of course, maybe the extra attention this week is my fault.

"Today on Alex 4 All," he says, and still grins like he's in love with this reference. I'm proud of how strong he is for not being embarrassed, though I guess I have no right to pride anymore. "I'm on the set of *The Beautiful Scourge* with fellow E.V.A. student Sadie Sheraton-Hayes."

The camera pans out, and Sadie is standing next to him. I stare at her—Sadie at her desk, that is, not on the screen—but she won't make eye contact with me.

"Sadie," I whisper, and then, "Sadie," I say in my real voice when she doesn't respond.

"Miss McAllister-Morgan, be quiet during the presentation," Ms. Cannon says.

When Alex's face popped up the first time TALON popped up, I didn't think anything could feel worse.

This is definitely worse.

TALON ends, and I have to just sit there in my desk, next

to Sadie, as if I care about women's history when all I care about, right now, is *our* history.

Sadie and I have fought before, of course. Neither of us remembers it very well, but apparently when we were four, we had some heated battles about which Powerpuff Girl was the best (for me it was always Blossom, and for Sadie it was Buttercup). In fourth grade my feelings got hurt because Sadie got invited to Shauna Weber's birthday skating party and I didn't, and then in sixth grade Sadie acted strangely threatened when I got my period before she'd gotten hers.

All of that was kid stuff, though. Literally.

This is something new. I've known for a while that our talking-every-day best-friend-ship had the expiration date of going off to college, but with me busy in Providence and her in Manhattan, we'd have other stuff to keep us occupied from missing each other. We'd see each other at Thanksgiving for the annual Sheraton-Hayes/McAllister-Morgan meal, and over Christmas breaks. We would have been fine.

But now I have to see her constantly, and she's already gone.

♥ ♥ ♥

I've somehow managed to make it this long without telling my parents about, well, *anything* that's going on, but I'm never going to make it through the weekend. During dinner I try bringing it up about a hundred times, but I can never fully form the words. Before I know it, the dishwasher is loaded and my parents are getting ready to watch TV.

I take a seat across from them before they have a chance to start watching whatever show's on tonight about solving crimes with forensic evidence.

"I have to talk to you guys," I say, and then something dawns on me. "Wait, has Mr. Wheeler already told you?"

"Told us what?" Darcy asks.

"There was a story in the *Crest*," I say. "About Alex."

"What about Alex?" Mom asks.

"We broke up again," I say. "I'm sorry, I should have told you sooner."

"Well, honey, it isn't that we don't care," Mom says, "because of course we do. But you really don't have to apologize. We've been seventeen. My senior year boyfriend—"

"Matt Hale?" I ask.

"Matt was sophomore year. Junior year was…oh my god. Darce, do you remember who I went out with junior year? Oh, but, right, senior year was when Paul and I broke up at least three times." Mom smiles. "And obviously Darcy had a lot of breakups to manage to date so many—"

"This is serious," I say.

"We're sorry," Darcy says, though she's still smiling as she rests her chin on Mom's shoulder. "What happened with the *Crest*?"

I explain the full situation, from when it came up at an

after-school meeting to Marisa's email, to the things Alex had said about Chaos 4 All to my decision made with Mr. Wheeler far away. I try to rush through it, because like with horror movies, the scariest parts are when everything's moving slowly.

"I'm so sorry." I wipe my eyes on my sleeve. "I didn't mean to destroy the reputation of a one-hundred-and-four-year-old tradition."

"I can't believe that's the worst article the paper has had in one hundred and four years," Darcy says.

I take a deep breath. "Also Sadie's really mad at me for the article, and I guess even more so for not telling her about being back together with Alex. And...maybe she was already mad at me for being a terrible friend."

"You aren't a terrible friend," Mom says very quickly.

"Maybe I am." I have to wipe my eyes on my other sleeve because the first one's already all wet. "I disappointed everyone."

"Honey, not everyone," Mom says. "Obviously Joe wasn't happy, and clearly Alex...but people screw up."

"I'm not supposed to let you down," I say.

"We're not let down," Darcy says. "And best friends fight. Sadie will be fine soon. Why are you still crying?"

"Don't make her defend herself for crying," Mom says. "Is there more going on, Jules?"

Darcy gets up from the sofa and crowds into the chair with me. "I know you're feeling a lot of pressure now, with your admission status hanging out there. But you've worked so hard. No matter what Brown says, you should be really proud of yourself."

"Right now the last thing I should be is proud." I lean my head against her. "I wanted to make it all worth it for you guys, and right now I haven't, at all."

"You wanted to make what worth it?" Mom asks.

"*Me.* I know you had to spend a lot of money for me to exist."

They do the thing where they exchange a look I can't decode. Being together for thirty years gives you communication superpowers.

"Julia McAllister-Morgan," Darcy says with a sigh. "We weren't in need of some return on our investment."

Mom gets up, and I'm afraid she's going to attempt a third person in this chair meant for one. Luckily she sits down in front of us and takes my hands. I wait to hear how they love me no matter what.

"When I was seventeen, I just wanted to get stoned and hang out with the drama kids," she says. "And Darcy—"

"I know, I know, dated twenty-five girls."

"I would *not* say 'dated,' and I'd definitely not say '*twenty-five*,'" Darcy says. "But you get the gist. You are definitely the most together anyone in the immediate family's been at seventeen."

"You told Paige and Ryan you couldn't have another kid because it was too expensive."

"Honey…" Mom laughs. "That has nothing to do with how you were conceived. You're in your thirteenth year of private school, after two years of private preschool. You're planning on attending *an Ivy League school.*"

"Kids are really expensive," Darcy says. "And our life is great. We didn't want to mess it up with dividing our time and money more. Of course we could have made it work if we wanted to."

"Do you promise?" I ask.

"We also say that to Paige and Ryan about anything we don't want to do," Darcy says. "Haven't you figured that out? It always shuts them up."

"They never stop otherwise," Mom says. "We've gotten out of so many things by claiming poverty."

"Anyway, you're my favorite thing we've spent money on," Darcy says. "Well, you or the espresso machine."

"Or the new pillow-top mattress," Mom says. "It's a toss-up."

"You're both so mean," I say.

Mom pulls me out of the chair so I'm sitting next to her on the floor. I expect Darcy to join us, but she just takes up more space in the chair. "You could publish a hundred bad articles and not get into any colleges at all, and we'd still think you were worth it, you know."

"Mom, I know you're trying to be nice," I say, "but that's almost literally my worst nightmare."

CHAPTER THIRTY-ONE

I get up on Saturday to walk dogs, of course, but just like Wednesday night, Alex isn't there. He was here almost constantly when we were broken up, and especially when we were "broken up," and so I know that his absence means something.

I miss him even more this time around, which I didn't realize was possible.

Mom and Darcy take me to the Huntington Gardens once I'm home, and I can tell they think the beauty and serenity of all the plants and flowers will make me forget about Alex, Sadie, and my failings. That's a lot to ask of orchids and succulents, though.

At home I check in on the blogs that "broke" Marisa's story. I'm relieved to see that the comments sections aren't exploding out of control any more than they do on any other unmoderated comments sections on the Internet. Most people have just taken the time to write something along the lines of "Who cares?"

If only that was the reaction within the halls of Eagle Vista Academy.

I know that technically there's no reason I couldn't go out, even if alone, but I feel like I should be grounded—even if Mom and Darcy don't. They go out to dinner just the two of them after I refuse to join (to be fair, they don't push me too hard), and then I'm left alone with all my thoughts and feelings.

Even the orchids and succulents would be better than those.

Em texts while I'm watching TV. **We're going to check out an art show at Pehrspace. Come with?**

I don't know who *we* includes, and I'm afraid to text to find out. I'm afraid to text back at all. Obviously Em believes in the magical healing power of time and breezes, but all I can picture is my whole group of friends—who mostly hate me at this point—staring when my name lights up on Em's phone. Nothing good could come from my phone at all these days, so I just turn it off.

It washes over me while two characters are kissing on-screen, and even though I know, I get out my organizer anyway. I open to today and stare at the heart I'd drawn. Right now I'm supposed to be with Alex. *With Alex.* And instead I'm alone watching TV actors make out.

After my run on Sunday, I finally respond to Em's text with an apology for not responding sooner. She replies with an offer to meet for coffee at Swork, but after ruining so many things I'm still not sure I deserve to be going out and having fun. Or even attempting it. I tell her I'm grounded, and that seems to settle it.

School somehow seems almost back to normal on Monday, with issues unrelated to me, that is. No one's clamoring to talk to me when I walk inside, but less people are staring at Alex today. I'll take the whole world hating me in exchange for that, considering it wasn't his fault.

The paper's back to covering its usual topics. I've never had so little to do with an issue, but I still save a copy of it, and not just because my name's in its usual spot on the masthead. The rest of the staff and Mr. Wheeler did a good job without Carlos, Marisa, or me. I try as hard as I can to not let that mean anything, though I fear it does.

I take an extra shift at Stray Rescue after school, because I know Mom will be home early enough to take care of Peanut and Daisy and start dinner. I'm sick of being alone with my thoughts about how much I've screwed up for people. At least I can do something good for dogs.

Darcy's already home when I arrive, which is almost unheard of on a Monday. In fact, there are a lot of suspicious things happening.

"Why are all these places set?" I ask, even though if the table leaf is in and places are set for seven, there's generally only one answer to that question. But I cannot believe with everything going on that the Sheraton-Hayeses would be on their way over.

"Paige and Ryan and the kids," Darcy says with her Come-on-Jules-this-is-obvious expression.

"I'm not even speaking to Sadie right now," I say. "I told you guys that."

The doorbell rings, and I know I won't be allowed to disappear upstairs into my room, so I just sit down in my usual chair and pretend to be busy looking at my phone. There's the usual amount of noise once everyone's inside, but I continue looking down until someone sits down next to me.

"Sometimes," Sadie says, "you're a big baby. And you should have told me about Alex, no matter what's going on with the *Crest* and with TALON. And the story about Chaos 4 All was...well, it was really mean. But I'm sorry. I don't think I did anything wrong? But I knew it would hurt your feelings, so I guess I did think so."

"Okay," I say, but slowly and softly, because if I'm really controlled, I might manage not to cry. A couple of tears drip down my face, though, which means the path's been officially cleared for as many tears feel like following. I'm pretty sure I've cried more in the past week than I did all of last year. Can that do permanent damage to your tear ducts?

"I need my own stuff too," she says. "I've tried to tell you that so many times, and you never get it. I'm so sick of being Paige Sheraton's Daughter."

"What about your hair?" I ask, and she laughs.

"Seriously! That's all I have. The hair's just because if I can't look perfect like Mom, I should at least look, like... *intentional.* I'm Paige Sheraton's Daughter, and I'm the Girl with the Hair. It *sucks.*"

"What do you mean? You're a million things more than that."

"You're my best friend. You don't count."

"I'm such a nerd compared to you," I say, and she bursts into laughter.

"What are you talking about? You're my freaking hero. I'm a goober."

"You were good on camera," I say.

"Oh no, what if it's hereditary!" She laughs. "Can we just not fight anymore? You're my person when I'm upset, so when I'm upset *at you*..."

"I know."

I hear what can best be described as a collective *Aw!* and look up to see our parents craning their necks around the doorway.

"Are you guys spying on us?" Sadie asks.

"Just the last thirty seconds or so," Darcy says.

"Forty-five, most," Paige says.

"Can we eat in my room?" I ask.

"Please?" Sadie adds. "Nothing's safe around you creepers."

"Yes, go," Mom says. "We'll bring dinner up in a few."

"But I object to *creeper*!" Ryan calls out.

♥ ♥ ♥

Sadie and I are still talking in my room when Paige checks in on us, hours later. We quickly get her to agree to let Sadie spend the night, even though it's a Monday.

"I'll have to get up really early tomorrow," Sadie says. "There's no way I can wear any of your clothes to school. You have to drive me home so I can get dressed."

"You can borrow whatever you want," I say.

"No offense, Jules, but I can't wear any of your skinny J.Crew prepster outfits. Even if I could fit into them." Sadie raises an eyebrow. "So what are we doing about Alex?"

"What are *we* doing? This isn't a group project. Could you just tell him that you fully believe that I thought the article would help him?"

"Of course," Sadie says.

"It's not so he'll take me back," I say. "I just don't want him to think someone would do that to him maliciously. Especially someone he trusted. Okay?"

"Jules! I already agreed!"

Mom leans into the room. "I know that it's late and I should tell you both to get some sleep, but you haven't had dessert and there's definitely leftover tiramisu downstairs."

"Yes!" Sadie jumps to her feet. "Lisa, tell us the truth. Did you guys plan a dinner just so Jules and I would have to hang out tonight?"

"My lips are sealed," Mom says, which sounds a lot like *yes* to me. "Anyway, it worked, didn't it?"

"No one could keep me and Jules apart for long," Sadie says. "Come on, Jules. Tiramisu!"

I follow her out of my room, but Mom grabs me by my shoulders as I walk by her. "What?"

"See? Everything's going to be fine."

"There's a lot that's still not fine," I say. "But thank you. If that's what you're looking for."

"That's *exactly* what I was looking for."

I hug her before joining Sadie downstairs in the kitchen.

♥ ♥ ♥

Tuesday is easier, even though I'm still suspended from my duties on the *Crest*. Sitting back and listening as everyone else pitches ideas, I feel as if I'm seeing what I couldn't before. If most of what we're doing is just to retain readership and compete with TALON, it's hard feeling like there's much effort left to put out the best news and information in the school. We added a lunchtime poll and a guest column—which always needs to be heavily, heavily edited—but I can't pretend those were really journalistic game changers.

The news does still matter, though, and I think it matters to the whole school even if they don't realize it. As a new idea descends upon me, I don't feel nervous and I don't worry if it's the right thing to do. I know it's the right thing to do.

I think about staying after our after-school meeting—it's clearly understood by the entire staff that our after-after-school meetings are a thing of the past—but I'm not sure big ideas are allowed during my suspension. And there's so much to get lined up; I can probably work faster and better without involving Mr. Wheeler.

I smile at that thought. Already I feel a lot like my old self again.

CHAPTER THIRTY-TWO

On Thursday morning I slip away from Sadie and Em while they're discussing potential Friday-night plans. Natalie's standing at her open locker, so I know I have at least a couple of seconds before she can run away.

"Hi," I say.

"What?" she asks without turning around. I can tell from her tone that she's well aware it's me.

"Do you have a moment?" I look down at my phone and double-check the time. "We have twelve minutes before the bell rings."

"Fine, Julia, I have a moment."

"Can we go somewhere we can talk?"

She sighs but slams her locker door. "Come on."

We start walking down the hallway together. I expect everyone to gape at us as we pass them, but it's possible our rivalry isn't as well known among the whole school as it is within our teams, even after the article.

We end up in the supply room. Considering that all the most recent times I've been in here were to make out with Alex, it seems an overly romantic spot for business negotiations.

"First I should say—regardless of how this goes—you'll be happy to know that...after the Chaos 4 All article, I think the *Crest* is going to calm down a little. I'm sure you'll be relieved to have less competition—"

"What are you talking about?" Natalie looks genuinely confused. "I never wanted less competition from you. I get more done because you're around, and I figured you felt the same. Would Batman even be Batman if the Joker wasn't running around screwing things up?"

"I'm not really familiar with the Batman canon," I say. "So...I don't know. Is that an accurate metaphor?"

"Not exactly, but you understand what I mean. I wasn't trying to ruin the paper for you, or for anyone else. We couldn't both be editor, and I assumed Mr. Wheeler would give the job to you—"

"Because you knew I would have pushed my way into the position no matter what?"

Natalie doesn't look as horrified at having her own words used again her as I would. If I had her poker face, I might actually be as capable of running the world as people tease me about.

"I was incredibly annoyed at you when I said that. You were trying to spy on us, and you did it in the most insultingly obvious way possible. It was offensive. No, that's not why I thought it was a given that Mr. Wheeler would pick you."

"Is it because we're neighbors?"

"You're *neighbors?*...Are you serious? You must have amazing stories."

I laugh. "Maybe not amazing, but, yeah, stories. My moms invite him over for dinner all the time. It's the worst."

"I had no idea, and that's—oh god. No, it's just that you're the one who can recite the history of the *Crest* off the top of your head, or explain to a freshman overall editorial voice and tone. You were a born editor. So I went off and made something else. That's all."

"It felt like you wanted to end us," I say.

"Looking back, I probably should have just talked to you about it," she says. "But we're not friends. I assumed that you were busy with your own things. And I didn't want to *end you.* TALON isn't why print media is on its way out."

"I still think the *Crest* is important," I say.

"Julia, I know," she says. "*Everyone* knows."

"My name is Jules," I say.

"Oh," she says. "I thought that was for your friends. I was trying to be respectful."

"Anyway, my point is that I think what we each do is important," I say. It hurts my soul somewhere deep down to compliment TALON to Natalie's face, but I can't deny that it's true. "Would you agree?"

Natalie shrugs. "Sure."

"And we definitely each do things the other can't," I say, even though that's also a little painful to say aloud.

"I miss the *Crest* sometimes," Natalie says. "I miss writing, at least."

"Yeah, TALON can't do the long-form pieces we do," I say. "But the visuals are great. And you're good on camera."

"Thanks," she says. "Initially, I actually thought..."

"What?" I ask. "Oh. Are you having an idea right now? Because I had this idea last night."

Natalie laughs. Today is literally the most I've seen her smile in all the years we've gone to school together. "Yes, Julia—Jules. We're having the same idea."

♥ ♥ ♥

We manage to get Mr. Wheeler and Ms. Baugher, TALON's faculty advisor, to meet with us after school that day. We each skip ASB to do so, but we decide that it's worth it. Natalie and I had spent lunch in the library, working on our pitch, but we didn't even get through our first bullet-point list when they agreed and said they'd figure out the details on how the combined teams would meet moving forward.

Natalie and I will have to both be in charge, which I suppose means neither of us is truly in charge, but this is the better choice for Eagle Vista, and for journalism, period. And, from the start, that's what I've been protecting.

Or at least it's what I should have been protecting.

"Jules, hang back, would you?" Mr. Wheeler asks as Natalie and Ms. Baugher leave his classroom.

I know that I still deserve to be reprimanded far beyond what's already happened. But I'm not looking forward to it, no matter how fair it is.

"This was a great idea," he says. "Good work."

"It was half Natalie," I say. "Only half me."

"Good half work, then," he says, and I manage a laugh with him because I know for Mr. Wheeler it's not a bad joke. "Jules, look, I was pretty angry last week."

"I know," I say. "I'm really so, so sorry that—"

"Let me finish," he says. "It was a rough week! I just lost my dad."

"I know," I say again. "I'm so sorry about that too."

"And I'm not saying that what you did was okay," he says. "But you've done a lot of great work for the *Crest* this year. You're one of the hardest-working editors we've had."

"Thank you."

"And..." He chuckles. "Well, I know how it is to want to get back at an ex."

"That isn't what happened!" I say. "I know that I should have asked you, and I know that we probably shouldn't have tied it into TALON. And, anyway, when it went to press... well, he wasn't my ex right then."

Oh my god, why am I telling Mr. Wheeler about my relationship status?

"Hang in there," Mr. Wheeler says as if nothing I said

verged on awkward. "Anyway, go home, play with your dogs, tell your moms I said hi."

"Mr. Wheeler," I say. "Your letter of recommendation..."

"I wouldn't change any of it," he says. "Okay?"

"Okay," I say. "I'm really sorry about your dad."

"Thanks," he says. "Now, I mean it! Get out of here. Go home."

I actually head down to ASB and sit next to Em, who's inexplicably been put in charge of taking notes while I was missing. I look over her shoulder to make sure there are more words than drawings in her notebook.

(There aren't.)

"I can take over," I tell her, switching on my phone to record.

"Thank god. Are you okay?"

I nod. "Are you doing anything after this? We can get coffee, or we can do something cooler, but you'll have to be in charge of whatever the something cooler is."

"Coffee is plenty cool, Jules," she says with a smile.

I doubt that, but it feels like the right thing to just pretend I agree. And after ASB, I hang out with Em, even though I have a pile of homework waiting for me in my backpack.

♥ ♥ ♥

The next day in fourth period, Mr. Wheeler leads us from his classroom to the TALON production room. Everyone finds a seat, and I try to act as if my far distance from Alex isn't planned.

"Some of you may have been filled in on this already," Mr. Wheeler says. "But I thought I'd have your two leaders give you the whole scoop. Jules and Natalie?"

We walk up at the same time, and I realize I'm actually happy to see all these faces who'd been part of the *Crest* up until this year. Right now they seem less like traitors and just like people.

Also, wait.

"Mr. Wheeler," I whisper. "What about my suspension?"

"I think you made up for it," he says. "More than made up. Go ahead."

I take my place next to Natalie at the front of the room. Finally, we'll get to use more of the speech we wrote yesterday for our advisors.

"Ultimately, TALON and the *Crest* have the same goals," Natalie says.

"Sharing timely and interesting information to the Eagle Vista Academy student body," I say.

"Everyone in leadership roles," Natalie says, looking to me before glancing back at Ms. Baugher and Mr. Wheeler, "has decided that the best way to do this is to combine forces."

"TALON can tackle everything that's really visual, or that makes more sense to report on a Friday versus waiting until Monday," I say.

"The *Crest* can write longer articles, including some of the stories we do on TALON that can't go into as much depth as we'd like," Natalie says.

"Everyone on both teams is eligible to suggest ideas for anything," I say. "Though I'm never going on camera."

"We'll see about that, Jules!" Mr. Wheeler calls for some weird reason. I'm so relieved he's not mad anymore that I laugh.

The *Crest* team already pitched ideas this week, and of course TALON just aired their latest show this morning, so we won't fully work together until next week. Natalie says that we should film an intro, so all of a sudden there are video cameras pointed at the desks, and we're told to just look natural because they'll run voice-over on top of the footage later. I have no idea how to look natural in front of video cameras—I can barely take successful selfies—but I like the look of this room. There are a lot of people who care in here.

When the bell rings, I end up walking out of the room at the same time as Alex. Our elbows crash as we aim for the doorway simultaneously.

"Sorry," I say.

"Hey, we're in hurries," he says. "You've got a salad calling your name in the cafeteria."

I smile at him. "Are you okay with...all of this? Should I have warned you?"

"Natalie warned me," he says.

"Oh," I say. It's not the first time I wonder if Alex might like Natalie, but it's the first time it feels like it's fair for him to. If I were a more generous person, I might even want him to.

Alex grins at me. It's good he can't read minds. "And, yeah. I'm okay with it."

"I miss you," I say, and it's basically out of my mouth before it hits me that I said it and didn't just think it. It's hilarious I thought Alex not being telepathic would mean he wouldn't know what I was thinking. "I'm sorry, I shouldn't have—"

"Jules," he says, and I'm waiting for him to say, *I miss you too.* "It's okay."

Right now that feels good enough. Almost, at least. Actually, no! It doesn't at all. But it's nice he's grinning again.

CHAPTER THIRTY-THREE

Now that the *Crest* and TALON are one, I thought the only thing I'd fixate on would be my impending news from Brown, but Alex is still taking up a lot of brain space. We've had real conversations every school day since the merge. None have been romantic—one was about how I overheard Mr. Wheeler on the phone saying that he *rocked out* at a Belle and Sebastian concert downtown, two were about cafeteria food, and several have been about Topics in Economics—but I still hope they each mean we're slowly finding our ways back.

Even if we're not, it's good not feeling like he hates me. I don't know if he'll ever believe that my intentions were 100 percent pure—and considering TALON was involved, I guess they really weren't—but maybe that doesn't matter as much now. It's strange what a big deal the story was and then how quickly it's blown away, just like Em said it would.

I approach Natalie, because I now see her as my equal or am at least attempting to. I'm convinced she'll fight me or, worse, look incredibly smug as I talk, but she does neither. And maybe it's just because my whole plan might only serve to make me look bad and remind people of something better forgotten, but Natalie not only agrees to my plan, but offers to help.

♥ ♥ ♥

By Friday morning I am feeling exactly the opposite of my emotional state the day our Chaos 4 All article hit the figurative newsstands. Considering how that turned out, hopefully the knot of anxiety in my stomach is a good sign.

"I meant to text you last night," Sadie says, sitting down right as the bell rings. I can't believe I'm only minutes away from appearing on screens across the entire school. Considering that the segment went a little differently than I'd planned, I have the urge to text Natalie—yes, I now occasionally have to text Natalie—and tell her to cut it, if there's still time.

If there's not time, maybe Carlos could show his butt again.

"Are you listening to me?" Sadie asks.

"Sorry, what were you going to text?" I whisper back.

"Mom and I were talking last night." Sadie rolls her eyes, but I know her well enough to spot that there isn't much behind this gesture. I still make a sympathetic face. "We're going to tour NYU again on a long weekend trip soon, and she says you can come with us."

"Miss Sheraton-Hayes," Ms. Cannon says with a sigh. "Please be quiet."

The TV screen descends, but despite what's coming, I manage to sneak a look at Sadie and mouth, *I'm in!*

TALON kicks off with its usual welcome from Natalie, then Kevin's segment showcases the titular Eagle Rock that gives this part of town its name, and Alex speaks with members of the Los Angeles Historical Society.

And then, it's me.

"Oh my god, Jules!" Sadie shrieks.

"Miss Sheraton-Hayes. Please."

"I'm Julia McAllister-Morgan, editor of the *Crest*," I say on-screen. I'm still not sure I'm built for on-camera life, but I don't look as washed-out as I'd feared. Apparently lighting can do great things. "We recently printed an article about TALON's online stats, which we have since retracted. I wanted to extend a personal apology to all staff and faculty members of TALON—which the *Crest* has since partnered with—for casting doubt onto your success. The level of research and verification was not up to the *Crest*'s usual standards, and I apologize for that as well, on top of pledging that our investigative journalism will never be printed without comprehensive confirmation."

I know what's coming next and am relieved to see that on-screen I'm not blushing the way I am positive I am right now. Luckily Sadie is watching my on-screen self too intently to notice and therefore point that out, loudly.

"Lastly, I want to deliver a personal apology to someone who was implicated most harshly in our piece, Alex Powell. There was no reason to tie your past into an article about TALON."

"Alex," I say, looking right at the camera, "I'm incredibly sorry for any false information we distributed about you. I never would have printed the story if I thought that it would hurt you."

The filmed me pauses for a split second. When this happened, I'd expected Natalie to bark at me for taking too much time or going off script. Amazingly, she didn't.

"I hope you'll forgive me because...I still Want 2 B Ur Girl."

Thankfully, I look embarrassed for saying it. But I also look sincere.

"Um, back to you, Natalie."

The *um* may have killed whatever professionalism I had left after parodying a Chaos 4 All song title, but I'm glad that it's out there. The apology and declaration, that is, not the *um*. I'll have to work on that before I go on camera again.

"Oh my god," Sadie says, once Natalie's back on-screen. *"Oh my god."*

There are a lot of murmurs, not just Sadie's whisper-proof voice. I don't know where to look, so I just look straight down at my desktop.

"Class," Ms. Cannon says with a heavy sigh. "Please pay attention."

We manage to get through the rest of TALON, and then

the rest of class. By now I don't know what to do with myself, so I just make a beeline for my locker and try not to notice that a lot of people are staring at me.

"That was amazing," Sadie says, right behind me. "You're so brave."

"I don't know why I said it, and then I don't know why Natalie kept it in."

"It's good for ratings!" Sadie laughs. "I'm kidding! It was perfect."

"I realized something," I say. "I want him back. If it's even possible."

"*Obviously*," Sadie says.

"So I'm being proactive," I say. "I'm proactive about everything else in my life. I should be on this too."

"He's coming over," Sadie whispers, and for the first time ever, it's a real whisper. The importance of the situation must have dialed her voice back. "Tell me everything later."

She slips away, and I try to casually finish switching out books from my locker. I'm not great at trying to act casual, so I have a feeling it might not be going over the way I intend.

"Hey," Alex says.

I turn around. "Hi."

He steps in close to me. "I want to tell you that . . . I believe you, Jules."

"About what?" I ask.

"You wouldn't have published that story if you thought it would hurt me."

"No," I say. "Never."

"I flipped out because…this is embarrassing." He takes a deep breath, and then lets it out. "That song was the biggest thing I was ever a part of. So to find out it wasn't actually anything—"

"You didn't know?" I ask. "At all?"

"Shit, no. I thought we magically got famous because we worked so hard and had a great song. I was naïve, I guess."

"You weren't naïve," I say. "The whole world believed it. It sounds like only a few people knew the truth."

The bell rings, but we smile at each other in a way that says we both don't care about tardiness in this moment.

"I still don't know who I am," he says. "I already didn't know, and now I feel like I know less."

"You don't have to know everything right now," I say. "You're only seventeen."

"You're the same age as me, and you know everything," he says.

"Not everything. This year's been…" I laugh. "Weird. Because of you, and TALON, and…and just *life*. I thought this whole year would be the paper and getting into college."

I take a deep breath, and then I lace my fingers through his. "When the year started, I knew what I wanted, and now… well, I'm less sure. But you—"

"Yeah, Jules?"

"I want to be with you," I say. "I miss you, and I don't want to miss you anymore. And I might still screw up, and

I'll probably still be crazy about the paper and now about TALON, and—"

"I feel like by now you should know that I like how crazy you are," he says. "I want to be with you too. Which is way more impressive, because I know *way less* what I want."

I slip my hands around his neck and rise up on my tiptoes. Everything I feel right now should be Alex, but I hear footsteps coming down the hallway. They sound suspiciously like teacher footsteps.

"Shhhh," I tell Alex, and we duck behind the end of the row of lockers until the footsteps are past us.

Amazingly, this works. I'm still on my tiptoes, and now Alex's arms are snug around my waist. We fit together as if we never didn't. A kiss shouldn't mean anything that words haven't already said, but when Alex's lips meet mine, I know that he still Wants 2 B My Boy.

who responded to me via email or social media about taking smarty-pants classes at your good high schools.

Thank you to my father, who passed away while I was finishing this book, for so much love, as well as the frequent comparisons to Mary Tyler Moore. Lastly, thanks to my mom, Pat Spalding, for her constant support and friendship.

ACKNOWLEDGMENTS

Thank you so much to the incredible Pam Gruber. You were the perfect editor to work with on Jules. A huge thank-you to the whole team at Poppy/Little, Brown, especially Jane Lee, Hallie Patterson, Leslie Shumate, Pam Garfinkel, and Farrin Jacobs.

Thanks, as always, to my amazing agent, Kate Testerman. You keep me as calm as I'm able to be, which is no small job, and your enthusiasm makes the scary parts of this process a heck of a lot easier.

Thanks to my amazing early readers and note givers: Robin Benway, Jasmine Guillory, Courtney Summers, Christie Baugher, and Sarah Skilton. Lots of extra gratitude to Christie for writing Chaos 4 All's biggest hit! Thank you so much to Rochelle Hartson, Lauren Kalb, and Ashley Denault for information about Brown University. Thanks to everyone